SAVAGE SCREAM!

Sundance ran to the lower end of the arroyo; he crouched, putting his hand over his eyes and not looking directly at the crimson sun.

Now he caught the drum of many hooves, and next, fierce war whoops. Out of that brilliant, blinding sunlight a line of wild riders broke, heading straight for the white camp, screaming bloodthirsty cries.

They zigzagged as they came, reckless in their insane speed. Naked to the waist, their torsos gleamed. And now they were close enough so Sundance could see their fierce faces. The streaks on their faces were black. Their war paint—the color of Death.

HONCHO

Jack Slade

LEISURE BOOKS ∞ NEW YORK CITY

A LEISURE BOOK

Published by

Dorchester Publishing Co., Inc.
6 E. 39th Street
New York City

Printed in the United States of America

ONE

When a heavy-caliber bullet shrieks within an inch of a man's ear, he does one of two things.

He freezes with fear, paralyzed by the specter of sudden death, his muscles unable to respond within the vital instant following the shock. That vital breath in which whoever means to kill him takes slightly more accurate aim and the next slug rips through his brain, the end of all things. The rider sags, his startled horse swerves, dashes off, and the still-warm body of what had shortly before been a living, breathing human being, falls from his saddle.

Or—

Jim Sundance didn't even use that flash of time. He had thrown himself sideways off his big appaloosa's back, landing with a jolt in the blood-red mud of the Choctaw Plains in the south of Indian Territory.

The following bullet, meant to finish him off, whined through the hot air; if he'd hesitated a wink of the eye, his earthly existence would have come to an end, then and there. By instinct, he knew what would come next. Since whoever it was had attempted to shoot him off his horse, now the marksman would try to fill him with lead as he lay, the wind knocked out of him by the hard fall from his saddle.

A couple more rifle bullets kicked up red dirt where he'd landed. But he was rolling fast; there were some rocks thrusting up from the surface, and then he was behind them, hugging Mother Earth for dear life.

Now, more guns crackled. But keeping low as he did, the bullets hit the boulders, showering him with shale.

Realizing they had missed him, they began trying for Eagle, but Sundance hadn't forgotten to slap the appaloosa hard on the rump, and the Nez Percé stallion knew what to do. He was already galloping full-speed toward a ragged line of cottonwoods that followed the winding course of a creek not far away.

Breath rasping, Sundance felt for his Navy Colt .44-caliber revolver. It was a relief to find it hadn't jogged from its holster when he had whirled through the air; he usually kept it shoved well down into its case, and the trigger had caught in his belt. He wished he had his Henry rifle, but he'd had no time to jerk it from its socket when he left his seat. He had his long, special Bowie knife, but that was of no use at the moment; it was really for in-fighting, though he could throw it with deadly accuracy under the proper circumstances.

He checked the heavy revolver, and it seemed to be undamaged. He cocked it, and held it; he was in top physical condition, and quickly recovered his wind. Above all, he stayed calm, figuring his chances, the odds. The timber along the stream wasn't far, and he might be lucky enough to zigzag into it before they could find him with their death lead. Or maybe he wouldn't be so lucky.

He felt something warm and damp running down his bronzed right cheek, irrigating the scar where a Crow arrow had once slashed his flesh. Sundance's hide was the color of an old penny; he had a typical Cheyenne Indian's face, hatchet-nose, thin, grim lips.

And this made the contrast much more startling, for his hair was the color of new wheat.

Jim Sundance was a half-breed; his father, Nick Sundance, as he'd chosen to call himself, had been an English remittance man who had elected to live with the Indians, adopting their ways. Nick had married a Cheyenne princess, a chief's daughter, and Sundance had been their beloved son. They'd kept him with them as they roamed over the vast wilds of the West and Southwest. The sire had taught his boy a great deal, educated him in white man's ways, and Jim had a genius for learning, particularly the languages of the various tribes; he could speak fluent Spanish, some French as well as English and many savage dialects. Also, the universal sign language came in handy throughout the regions west of the Missouri . . .

Sundance touched his cheek, gripping his colt as he pancaked behind a barricade of rock. It wasn't a bullet scrape. He'd been gashed by a sharp stone when he'd landed. The fall had knocked his battered old Stetson off, and it lay where it had come down after sailing through the air.

"Sundance!"

He alerted. His hearing was as keen as any animals, and he placed the voice, which had an unusual timbre, though he couldn't immediately identify what it was. But whoever had sung out to him was hidden in a clump of chaparral and jagged rocks on a slight rise to the southeast of his position.

He did not answer but lay as still as if that first one had really killed him. He had an Indian's stoic patience for such work. A savage would lie in wait for long periods of time, waiting, watching for prey. He would not even twitch.

"Jim Sundance!" came the voice again. And now he realized it had a resonant sound to it, as well as an unusual timbre. Whoever was holed up in the nest must be using a small megaphone of the type Army officers sometimes employed to relay commands during a noisy battle, when gunfire might drown out the ordinary human voice.

Sundance lay quiet.

He was hoping they might think he was dead; he knew more than one had fired at him, for besides the first heavy rifle's sound, he'd identified a couple of carbines, which had a lighter explosive force.

The blood flow wasn't serious; it was already checking itself.

He lay with his cheek against the ground; through veiled eyes, he could just make out the outer rim of the nest from which they'd attempted to make the kill. But they evidently couldn't see him from the point they had chosen for the ambush.

He eased the cocked Navy Colt bit by bit so it lay along his hip; he kept his finger in the trigger guard, and the weapon was ready for instant use.

It was impossible for him to make any careful

study of the ambush spot; that would have meant exposing himself fully. As long as he stayed where he was, he was safe for the moment.

Then, around one end of the nest, Sundance saw two men, one tall, thin, rawboned, the other stouter. Both gripped Winchester carbines and were watching the point where he was hidden. They were strangers to him; he'd never seen either before. But he recognized the type. They wore Stetsons, sweated shirts, riding pants, and cartridge belts with Frontier Model Colt's .45 revolvers in open, supple holsters, and hunting knives in sheaths at back ribs. They held the carbines as though familiar, as experts would—Sundance could tell.

They kept watching the low rock outcrop behind which Sundance lay, frozen as if in death.

Gunfighters—or gunmen, fellows who would hire out to the highest bidder. A cowboy, no matter how wild and rollicking he might be when in his cups, had an entirely different air about him, though he might dress the same. To a waddy, guns were a necessity at times, but they weren't the chief tools of his trade.

He watched, most carefully. They might open fire as soon as they reached a point from which they could see his head and upper torso.

They made a pretty good stalk; one kept off to the left while the other was on the right. They had a slight disadvantage, for they were facing the sun and had to squint, but each held his Winchester at the ready and could raise it and fire in a flash.

Sundance let them draw closer, closer. They kept craning up, trying to see more of their prey, and he heard one say, "Buck, I see blood on his cheek. I think Franz got the cuss."

"Maybe. But maybe he's just knocked silly. Franz says he's a tough, smart breed, so watch him."

Jim Sundance never moved a muscle as they came at him.

And now they were close—too close! Through lowered lashes he could make out their features; one had a broken nose and an adenoidal open mouth, teeth yellowed by chewing tobacco, and he needed a shave.

"Put a finisher into him, Murph," advised Buck. "He looks kinda nasty."

"Yeah, we better be sure." The carbine was rising to take a steady bead at Sundance's head.

The dead came to life with a sudden, murderous lash, like a big alligator, apparently somnolent, attacking with merciless fury.

Sundance's Navy Colt belched metal and flame, and Murphy's carbine exploded but the bullet ploughed dirt two feet away from Sundance, and Murphy's body went down hard; the man was dead before he thudded on the ground.

Buck wasted a precious instant, to glance unbelievingly at his pard; he yelped, startled, and then pulled trigger.

But he was too late. Sundance wasn't there any more. He was crouched like a cougar ready to spring, and he took aim with icy precision. The heavy revolver bullet drove into Buck's chin, drove upward, smashing through the palate into the man's brain.

The carbine flew from his relaxing grip. Sundance made a grab for it, caught it, and dropped back behind his low barricade in the nick, for a heavy rifle slug whistled over his lowered head. The man still concealed over there had tried again. Only Jim Sundance's incredible, trained speed had saved him.

Now he had the carbine; he worked the mechanism, pumping another cartridge into the firing chamber, and lay flat, peeking out from the right of the rock outcrop. He saw the sunlight glint on a burnished, long rifle barrel and took a snap shot at it.

He knew he'd missed, for the rifle was hastily drawn back.

The explosions of the guns died off; bluish powder smoke drifted lazily toward the torrid sky. Sundance waited, unmoving, after he'd worked the lever, putting another load into the carbine.

It seemed like a long wait. A flock of geese veered off as they sighted the men below; they were wise to the ways of hunters.

But the wilderness was again peaceful, quiet; there was only a faint breeze stirring the air.

Finally, the unpleasant voice spoke again through the megaphone:

"I told those idiots to watch carefully!" No pity, only impatience at the stupidity of his gunhands.

And now Sundance thought he had it, that accent. Instead of "watch" the man had said "vatch."

"Sundance, can you hear me?"

Sundance didn't reply. The magnified voice warned, "Sundance, keep away from Ft. Smith!" There it was again; instead of "away," the "w" was slurred, and it sounded like "avay."

German, from the imperious tone. "Franz," as Murphy had called him when he'd spoken his last words to Buck.

He'd known such men before in his long and checkered career. They couldn't tolerate slower minds or mistakes, which irritated them.

Sundance suddenly opened fire with the carbine he'd snatched. He threw bullets in a covering line at the chaparral-screened nest.

Emptying the weapon, he threw it aside, leaped to his feet and dashed full-tilt, bent low, zigzagging, running the gantlet.

His fire had kept the unseen enemy down; Sundance had only a short distance to reach the growth along the creek. A bullet missed his body by inches, another kicked up dirt just behind him. Then he dove into the bush.

TWO

Sundance scrabbled through the undergrowth, oblivious to thorns that tore at his clothes and flesh. He made it behind a thick cottonwood bole, and stood up; he was breathing fast, from the hard run and exertion. But his brain was cool, clicking.

Eagle wasn't far off. The powerful appaloosa stallion's muzzle was wet; he'd drunk from the creek, and was cropping green grasses along the bank, swishing his tail to keep flies off his spotted rump.

The horse carried the man's bedroll, and besides that, two larger parfleche bags, one long and cylindrical, the second rounder. These special bags held Sundance's equipment, bow and quiver of arrows, his Cheyenne headdress, each feather spelling an enemy killed in battle, though a couple were for slaying grizzlies in hand-to-hand combat.

But now he wanted his repeating Henry rifle. He snatched it from the socket, threw a cartridge into the firing chamber, and bellied back until he could see the fringed clump to the southeast from which the two men, Murphy and Buck, had emerged, and the point from which the megaphoned voice had come.

Indians always picked up their wounded and dead when it was at all possible, even though it might mean they might be hurt or killed in the process. There was a slight hope that maybe the fellow they'd called "Franz" might at least check his aides.

But this hope quickly faded. Franz wasn't exposing himself.

He was shouting through his megaphone again, shouting to Sundance.

"Sundance! Sundance! I know you can hear me. Keep away from Fort Smith. You won't be so lucky next time!" "Avay," instead of "away". . .

The grim Indian countenance didn't change expression; and Sundance didn't reply. He lay snugged to the ground, the Henry up and at his shoulder, cocked, ready to trigger.

Far in the hazy sky, black specks planed slowly in a wide circle which diminished as the vultures dropped closer. It was a marvel how they could so quickly spot death. Sundance had often wondered at it. Was it keen eyesight, beyond the understanding of man?

Stoically, he waited. The man didn't call to him again. He kept studying the chaparral, but sharp as his trained eyes were, he detected not the slightest stir.

Maybe he could draw fire, marking his target. He pulled trigger, once, twice, again. The leaves of the bush were whipped by his bullets, but Franz didn't bite at the bait. And then, Sundance caught the drum of receding hoofs. There was a long slope cutting off his field of vision. Soon, he sighted reddish dust, rising slowly to the warm sky. It followed the southern line of the slope.

No use wasting ammunition; he couldn't possibly make a hit.

He pondered pursuit. Eagle could overtake any other critter, but it would mean riding full-tilt, and chances were that Franz would figure on this and lie in ambush, with a good chance of hitting Sundance or the larger target, the appaloosa.

The two silent forms of the dead gunhands lay there, baking in the sun. Bluebottle and other flies were already swarming over them, and the buzzards had dropped very low.

Sundance went to the water and lay flat, drinking. Then he shed his buckskin shirt, decorated with fine beadwork, his brown denim pants, his moccasins. Naked, he bathed in the creek; the Cheyennes were clean and bathed daily, even in midwinter.

He checked again. Except for the insects and the buzzards, some of them now on the ground, approaching the corpses with their awkward gait, ugly heads bobbing, the wilderness seemed deserted. He gathered dry sticks and made a small fire which gave off little smoke. He rolled a cigarette and smoked as he fixed a piece of jerked beef on a sharp stick before the blaze, and put a little water on to boil in the small pan he carried with him. He had hardtack, and with the meat and hot coffee, it would make a satisfying meal.

He squatted on his haunches, Indian-fashion, as he ate. He would put a chewable size of the jerky in his mouth and cut it off with his razor-sharp Bowie knife.

When he'd eaten, he fixed another cigarette, and drew a folded paper from his pocket. He had read the note several times, and now he studied it once more:

"Dear Mr. Sundance: General George Crook was passing through Fort Smith on his way north. He told me you specialize in finding and freeing white captives from the Indian tribes. I must talk to you. I fear my dear son, Roland, who is only eleven, has been captured and taken by the savages into the depths of Indian Territory. Roland is a typical boy. He loves adventure and the West fascinated him. He told me he wanted to be a cowboy, an Indian fighter, a buffalo hunter, and read everything he could about the Frontier. He liked guns and he was bored by his studies. We had sent him to a private school in St. Louis, and he ran off; he has an allowance, and we know he bought a railroad ticket to Little Rock, Arkansas, then took a stage line to Ft. Smith. After that, we could find no trace of him. He may well have crossed the Arkansas and wandered into the wilds of the Territory, then been caught by one of the many Indian tribes. There has been no ransom demand.

"I write this to you secretly; my husband, Adolf Froleiks, isn't Roland's father. My first husband, Jean Bouchet, was killed in the Franco-Prussian War, and I came to the United States, hoping to recover from the shock: I met Adolf, and remarried. When I told him General Crook had recommended you, he grew very angry and forbade me to get in touch with you. I don't know why, but please contact me carefully if and when you reach Ft. Smith.

We live at 34 Fifth Street, a short distance from the Arkansas River. I will pay you well. Please, I beg of you, help me. Anxiously, Simone Froleiks. P.S. I will pay you well, Mr. Sundance."

Simone, French, Adolf Froleiks, German. Franz, who'd led the drygulchers trying to kill Sundance, sounded German, too, though Americanized.

Jim Sundance was a well-educated man. He knew something of the several German provinces which had been welded by Bismarck into the comparatively new German state. The south Germans, the Bavarians, and others, were usually good-humored, fine folks, but the dominant Prussians were arrogant and warlike, with no mercy for the weak.

He didn't understand, either, why Simone's husband was so set against her asking Sundance's help. It was a mystery he would attempt to solve.

He had no intention of camping here, near the spot where he'd nearly been killed by Franz. He doused the coals of the little fire, covered the ashes with dirt, wiping out all sign. Mounting Eagle, he forded the shallow creek to the north side and rode along the bank for a few hundred yards to hide his trail.

He found a hidden spot on a slight rise not far from the winding stream, unsaddled and rubbed down Eagle, and spread his bedroll under a large southern pine, placing his weapons by his side; he would come alert at an instant's warning and be ready to defend himself.

It took some time before he fell asleep. He had so much to remember, so much to think about, and most of it was sad. He had long ago realized the fate of the Indian was sealed. The dominant whites were greedily seizing all the great regions of every tribe.

His mother had been a chief's daughter of the *Hevataniu*, the Southern Cheyenne, their particular band being the *Is-sio-me-tan-iu*. And he'd traveled everywhere, from the Canadian border into Mexico, had crossed the Rockies and Sierras and gazed upon the mighty Pacific. His fame had spread, not only among the Indian tribes, but throughout the white world as well, for he sent all the money he could earn to Washington, to be used by a trusted attorney in what Sundance feared was a losing war, to gain better terms for the defeated redmen. And now, his woman, whom he had so loved, Barbara Colfax, was also in Washington, D.C., assisting in the fight. Barbara had been a beautiful white society girl but had chosen the Indian way of life.

But that was over for her. Sundance had confronted General George A. Custer at the Battle of the Little Big Horn, along with the paladin of the Sioux, the Oglalla Chief Crazy Horse, Pizi, Gall, and the Hunkpapa War Chief, urged on by Sitting Bull, mèdicine man as well as warrior. The Cheyenne Chief Two Moon and other great warriors had taken part in the battle, leading 5000 infuriated braves into battle against Custer's 7th Cavalry. They had killed Long Hair, Custer—though his hair had been cropped short at the time of the fight. And they had wiped out over 200 men in Custer's immediate contingent, along with some of Major Reno's and Captain Fred Benteen's sections. About half the 7th Cavalry had died or been wounded.

It was the greatest victory ever by the Indians against the whites. But Sundance had known immediately it was the end for the tribes. The white men would step up their campaigns to exterminate the redmen.

So, he had ordered Barbara Colfax to Washington, to live again as a white woman, and he would send her monies to fight for Indian rights, to get them a better deal on the reservations they were consigned to, where they were mercilessly cheated by the infamous Indian Ring . . .

His first great appaloosa, Eagle I, had been belly-shot during the fight at the Little Big Horn, and sadly, Sundance had been forced to end the animal's suffering. He'd hurried to the Nez Percé and bought and trained another big appaloosa, whom he also named Eagle.

Even Chief Joseph, of the Nez Percé, who had never fired a shot in anger at the whites, was worried. They were seizing more and more of the Nez Percé lands.

Sundance had returned to the vicinity of the Little Big Horn, the Greasy Grass as the Indians called the river. From a safe spot, he'd watched his old friend, General George Crook, who had been driven back, after Crazy Horse, with only 1000 braves, had struck his advance guard in a cunning ambush. Crook had had 1500 men, 1200 of them whites, infantry, cavalry, artillery; his supply train had stretched behind him for over a mile, and he had 300 Snake and Ree Indian scouts as well. Crook had suffered his first and only major defeat on the Rosebud. He'd gone into camp on Goose Creek to bury his dead and see to his wounded. While awaiting reinforcements, Crook had gone hunting the mountains, his favorite pastime . . .

Crook's serious defeat had left a vacuum into

which General Custer, commanding the 7th Cavalry, had ridden to his death.

It had been August before Crook finally arrived at the Greasy Grass. Generals Alfred Terry and Gibbon, with Crook, had marched up and down again, seeking the Sioux and Cheyennes, but they had split into small bands and disappeared in the foothills of the Rockies. Reservation Indians, who had taken part in the battle, had hastily returned. No Indian would admit being at the Little Big Horn, for the whites were like infuriated hornets, and would have hung any brave who had taken part in the fight.

And Sundance had been right. For General Nelson Miles had equipped his forces for Arctic warfare, and hunted down the Sioux and Cheyenne in the dead of the worst winter ever known. The Indians couldn't ride in such deep snows; they couldn't move their children, squaws and old folks.

Sitting Bull, Chief Gall and many braves had slipped over the line into Canada, where the Grandmother, Queen Victoria, gave them haven. In the spring, Crazy Horse, most feared of all Sioux, had surrendered his starving, naked band of Oglallas, and now word had reached Sundance that Chief Joseph had been forced to take the warpath for the first time. Joseph hoped to escape into Canada and join Sitting Bull . . .

Yes, it was Armageddon for the American Indian.

A night wind had sprung up, and Sundance pulled up his blanket against the chill. He had much in his memory—too much. He had loved Barbara Colfax, but she was far away. Maggie Montelle, too, had been a wonderful wife to him. He'd taken her into the Mexican mountains with him, to palaver with

Apache chief friends. She'd loved the rough life, and they'd been very happy. His Indian friends, aware she was his woman, would never harm her, but when Sundance and most of the warriors had been away for several days on a long hunt for meat, Mexican bandidos had crept up on the hidden camp, led to it by some traitor. They had killed the few men on hand, raped the women and slain many of them. Maggie had died, too. But she hadn't been raped; she'd shot herself.

Sundance was a vigorous man. It was a long time since he'd been with a woman.

He slept, then, and awoke with the first dawn. He bathed, checked his gear and Eagle, who was trained as a watchdog as well as a warhorse. He made a small fire and boiled water, threw in a handful of coffee; then he saw a slight movement in the shallows where he'd been swimming. Quietly, he drew his Bowie knife and soundlessly crept to the bank of the stream. A large carp-like fish had returned to its nest, where it was laying its eggs to spawn.

With a swift movement, he half-stabbed, half-scooped the fish to the bank. It was a big one, with plenty of meat on it. He cleaned and gutted it, hung it up to broil before his fire. It made a hearty meal for him, though the meat was rather soft, without too much flavor.

He cinched his high-pronged saddle on the appaloosa, and arranged his bedroll, fastened on the parfleche bags so they rode behind him on the horse's spotted rump. He shot his Henry rifle into the boot, checked his Navy Colt, covered his fire and sign, and started across the stream.

Then he drew back. He watched as an Indian family walked westward across the Choctaw plain. The father was in the lead, his squaw coming behind, carrying a papoose on her back; there were four other small children. They had an old pack donkey which a larger boy led, and they were no doubt going to visit friends or relatives somewhere in the great Territory.

They paid no attention to Sundance, even if they saw him, but walked with the steady, tireless gait of the Indian.

He resumed his ride northeast toward Ft. Smith. The Indian Territory had been of prime interest to Sundance. It was a huge reservation, studded with rivers and beautiful lakes. In the south sections, there were immense pine forests; as the mountains rose northward, there were many square miles of hardwoods, oak, hickory, ash, and there was also cypress in swamps; there were gum and elm forests, and 200 types of trees.

First, the whites had consigned the five "civilized" tribes, the Nations, to the area, the Cherokees, the Choctaws, Chickasaw and Creeks, the Seminoles from Florida and south Georgia, though some of the Seminoles had escaped into the Everglades and set up there.

But now, the Osage, and the Arapahoe had been pushed in; also, as they were subjugated, the Comanches and Kiowas.

The Nations had their own police and courts and could punish Indian wrongdoers as they pleased, though white men were not under this jurisdiction, and the Territory had become a haven for the worst murderers, bandits and horsethieves in the West.

The only jurisdiction exercised over whites was by

Judge Isaac Parker, whose court was in Ft. Smith. His deputy federal marshals would penetrate the wilderness, hunting down outlaws wanted for the worst of crimes. It was a dangerous game; in some years, fifty percent of the deputies were ambushed and killed by the deadly game they hunted, for many outlaws preferred to shoot it out and chance dying, rather than face the stern Judge Parker and his hanging machine, which could drop a dozen men at once.

Sundance had no fear of Indians. It was the white murderers he must watch for. Plenty of them would gladly kill him to take the beautiful appaloosa he forked . . .

He had crossed the Red River, the Little River, and wound his way through the mountain passes, always aiming for Ft. Smith.

The beauty of the land was stunning, with the great forests, abounding with plenty of game he could kill with bow and arrow, and use as sustenance. He found berries and roots that were edible, and lived well.

He was in good shape when he prepared to swim Eagle across the Arkansas. He was a few miles above Ft. Smith when he crossed. He went into camp and considered what his best move would be. He intended to contact Simone Froleiks, but she had warned him that her husband was violently set against Sundance being called in to hunt for his stepson, Ronald.

Sundance had a typical Cheyenne face, black eyes, thin lips, and hide the color of an old penny. But that was all right. Indians were a common sight in Ft. Smith. But the big man's fame had spread throughout the Frontier. Too many people would know who he was on sight, though they hadn't ever met him.

His battered old Stetson wouldn't hide his hair, which flowed to his shoulders. Well, he'd crop it, it would grow again. He drew the long Bowie knife, perfectly balanced; it had been made in New Orleans by a master craftsman. He found a small whetstone in his saddlebag, spat on it, and honed the knife till it was sharp as a razor. With this, he cut his hair. A hunter's cap would hide his pate, and he'd look like a typical Indian hunter.

He'd been in Ft. Smith, and through Indian Territory. He'd visited the Cherokees at Tahlequah, in the northeast. The Osages had been squeezed in near them. Westward were Comanches, Kiowas, and Cheyennes, and others not on the Sioux reservations such as the Rosebud in the Dakota Territory.

It was near dusk when he stopped in a store and bought a dark-blue hunter's cap to cover his cropped hair. He had plenty of money, in his pockets and belt and stowed in his bags. Indians were a common sight in the town, and many worked at menial jobs. His next goal was a livery stable. He left Eagle in the road and looked in the front office. The owner had evidently gone home for the night, and an Indian wrangler sat at a small desk, with an oil lamp on it. He wore Levi's, an old gray shirt, and his black hair was cut short. From his general look, Sundance decided the wrangler was a Cherokee. He entered the office, and the wrangler rose, staring at him impassively. When he realized the customer was an Indian, his features relaxed.

Sundance spoke to him in Cherokee; he knew the

tongue, and many of them knew English, as they worked among the whites.

The wrangler's face grew animated as he replied, and gave his Indian name, Tall Littleman. Sundance ordered a rubdown, watering, plenty of fresh hay for the stallion when he was turned into one of the corrals in the rear. He paid in advance and gave Tall Littleman a substantial tip; he paid for a week ahead.

Then he swept off his cap. Tall Littleman's jaw dropped as he saw the flaxen hair. He was puzzled for a moment; then his eyes lighted up. "You—you are Sundance! The Indian's friend."

"Yes, I'm Sundance. You must promise not to tell anyone I'm here, Tall Littleman, for there are white enemies who might kill me in Fort Smith. And I've given you extra money so you will take good care of my saddle, my special bags and Henry rifle."

Tall Littleman would hide the gear in a rear loft, keep it covered. Nobody, not even his boss, Reilly, would know.

Sundance kept his Navy Colt and cartridge belt, the Bowie, and for his operations he kept on his moccasins. Leaving the livery after turning Eagle over to the Cherokee, he walked with long strides along N. 1st Street until he came to a small restaurant. He ordered a substantial meal, fried potatoes, steak, honey and biscuits, topped off with two slabs of dried-apple pie. He dawdled over the pie and several cups of coffee, smoking several quirlies. Paying the score, he went out.

Night had fallen and hundreds of lamps twinkled in the city. Street lights had been touched off. With his rapid gait, he soon came to Fifth Street, easily locating No. 34, a large house of two stories and two side wings, besides the rear kitchen. There were several chimneys for wood fires and to carry off smoke from stoves.

When he'd studied this from the front, he circled around to the rear. Servants were in the kitchens, cleaning up after the evening meal. In a wing on the far side, upstairs, were two lighted windows, probably a bedroom.

Only an Indian could move so silently; at the slightest sound, Sundance would freeze in the shadows. Finally, he peeped in at the lower corner of a window up front. Three lamps burned brightly in there. He saw comfortable chairs and rugs, tables, a desk, and a fire crackling in the hearth, though the windows were partly open.

A large man in a frilled white shirt open at the bull throat, dark trousers and fine leather slippers, sat, smoking a cigar. His side face was toward Sundance, and it was a strong, determined face, with a crisp brown mustache matching the closely cropped hair.

Sundance thought the mouth had a cruel twist to it, and he decided the man was an imperious character determined to have his own way in everything. Suddenly he dropped the map and rose; he had an erect, military carriage, an arrogant air.

Then he saw why the man had risen. A woman, with a beautiful figure showing through the silk robe she wore, had entered. "I've come to say goodnight, 'Dolf," she said. She approached and started to kiss him but he impatiently turned away his face.

"Goodnight, Simone. I've told you, you aren't to leave this house without my permission. Do you understand?"

"I understand—I understand fully."

"Just what do you mean by that?" he demanded, scowling at her.

"Nothing. I know you're very busy." With a nod, she left.

As she passed between a large lamp and Sundance, he could see the outlines of full bosoms, the charming curve of womanly hips. She wore her black hair in two braids down her back; her face was most pleasing, with cherry-red lips. She was a lure to any male . . .

" 'Dolf" must be Adolf Froleiks, her husband, who'd been so furious when he'd somehow learned she'd sent for Sundance.

A bell clanged from the front door, and a Cherokee Indian servant hurried to answer.

Soon, a man who at first glance reminded Sundance of a bad-tempered grizzly bear, strode into the parlor. Froleiks was tall, but the newcomer topped him by three inches, and was much heavier, though he moved with an animal-like quality.

"Well, Franz? Did you get him?"

Sundance could hear Franz cursing. "Nearly! But that redskin breed is an eel, Froleiks. We were laying for him on the Choctaw Plains, figured he'd have to come that way from Fetterman. I missed him by inches, and he killed two of my best boys, Buck and Murphy. Then I wasted time, waiting in ambush, thinking he'd trail me, but he was too wily for that. He got clear, clear away."

There it was. The "w's" sounded like "v's," "vasted," "avay," other words.

Sundance would never forget that voice which had

shouted at him through a megaphone.

He knew he'd come to the right place.

THREE

Crouched in the shadow below the window, Sundance listened. He heard Froleiks exclaiming in anger. "You'll have to get him in town, for he's sure to come here. Luckily our man at Fetterman got a look at Simone's letter or he'd have been here without us knowing. He can do us a lot of damage, Franz, negotiations have just begun and are in a delicate stage. That rascal Sundance has a lobby of his own in Washington, always working against the whites, to help the cussed redskins."

Franz sank into an easy chair, poured four fingers of whiskey into a glass, and drank it at a gulp. Froleiks tossed him a cigar, and the two began studying the map on the table. "Yeah, it's better'n than we thought," said Franz, as he traced several circles on the map with a stubby forefinger.

Sundance listened for a time but the men spoke in low tones, so he missed much of it. Franz was saying, "I was worn out, 'Dolf, when I finally got home. I had to sleep a while."

Franz had changed from trail clothes; he had on a dark suit, a blue shirt with a stringtie. His black hair was shaggy, as was his heavy beard. He had an overlarge face, with thick brows over quick eyes, red-rimmed by trail dust. The hand he used to trace details on the map was like a ham.

One tough hombre, thought Sundance. Froleiks and Franz behaved more like partners than master and assistant. Maybe Froleiks handled the politics and finer details, while Franz was field general.

"Why not hire some Indian scouts to smell him out?" suggested Froleiks.

"Never! All Indians love and respect Sundance. I got some real good, tough white gunhands who'll plug any redskin on sight, they hate 'em all. Expert Indian fighters, nothin' better."

Franz rose and poured another drink for himself, puffing on his cigar. The two moved off to a far corner, and lowered their voices. Sundance could no longer hear what they were saying, only the murmur of their voices. Froleiks was drinking now, with Franz.

Busy listening at the window, Sundance suddenly heard a twig crack near him. Somebody was coming along the house from the front, and Sundance saw him framed darkly against a street lamp.

"Hey, you, what you—freeze, cuss it!"

He heard the sound of a cocking revolver. With his unerring, unbelievable speed, he dove in at the man's legs; the gun exploded, the bullet burning the air over Sundance's lowered head.

The man went down hard, grunting as the wind was knocked out of him. Sundance drove a knee into the belly, wrested the Colt from the relaxing hand,

and tossed it into the shrubbery.

But they'd heard the shot in the front parlor. Franz was at the window, and he sang out, "Bernie, that you? What's wrong?"

But Bernie lay unconscious in the grass. Sundance had buffaloed him with the Navy Colt, and was already running toward the rear of the house.

He cut through to the next street, loped through shadowy yards between the lighted homes. He reached an alley and moved back to N. 4th, watching the front of Froleiks' home from a safe distance.

There were two saddled horses standing at the tie post. The giant Franz came from the other side of the place; he was carrying Bernie, who'd been waiting outside, and must have somehow chanced to see the unknown interloper at the window who had challenged him.

Sundance waited patiently. Franz laid his man on the porch and went back inside. It would have been interesting to hear what was being said in there, but he didn't dare go nearer now, with the alarm. In a short time, Franz reappeared. Froleiks came out, carrying a lamp. Franz threw a pitcher of water over Bernie's head, then held his aide and gave him a drink of liquor from a glass Froleiks handed him. Bernie was coming to now, and sat up. Then Franz half-carried him and lifted him to his saddle. Bernie gripped the horn with both hands, and Franz led his horse behind as he hit the street and swung off, riding slowly.

When they were gone, Froleiks went back inside and closed the front door.

Sundance figured it out. They might now know

he'd been there and had laid Bernie low, but a thousand to one Franz would fetch back men and post them as sentries around Froleiks' home, just in case. Huge as he was, Franz wasn't stupid. It was the only thing a smart general would do.

So, he knew he hadn't much time in which to act. He must contact Simone Froleiks, and he must do it at once, before Franz returned with sentinels.

Daring was part of Sundance's nature. Danger, to him, was a tonic without which he couldn't get along. Stealing closer, always in shadow, he closed in on the house again, this time from the other side, away from the parlor where he'd seen Froleiks and Franz. Crouching nearby, he could see two lighted rooms in the second story ell, which would be a bedroom, and he hoped it was Simone's. A great oak spread its branches inside the ell, and a glance told him he could scale it; a thick limb reached within easy distance of one of the lighted, open windows.

It was now or never, if he wanted to contact Simone. And what with Froleiks and Franz, the game was growing most fascinating to him.

He caught a lower limb and began to climb. The cartridge belt hampered him; he unbuckled it and hung it on a handy tree spur.

It wasn't far to the bedroom window he'd picked. He must first make certain it was Simone's though, and he sat on the limb, hanging with one hand to a higher branch. Now he could look through the open window. The pretty woman he'd seen downstairs was sitting in a chair by a bedside table, reading a book.

Now, she shook her braids, stood up, went to her bureau and picked up a framed photograph. She took this back and studied it for some time, then with a sad expression, returned it to its place.

He watched her bolt her door into the outer hall. Then she took off her negligée, and he saw she was clad in a paperthin silk nightgown revealing her charms.

She turned the lamp down but didn't blow it out; she left it burning low, a night light, and she turned down her covers and got into bed. She lay for a time, with her eyes open, on her back. Now, she closed her eyes, and Sundance still waited, hoping she would fall asleep quickly.

He waited as long as he dared, then slid through the open window and crouched on the rug. She didn't take alarm, but in a few swift steps he had reached her side and clapped a hand over her mouth so she wouldn't cry out. Her large eyes were violet; they opened very wide, staring up in fright at the grim hatchet face of the man.

"Don't be afraid," he whispered. "I'm Sundance. You sent for me. Keep your voice very low. Your husband sent men to kill me before I could get here."

He could feel her relax, and took his hand from her lips. "Sundance! You—you startled me. But I'm happy you've come."

He stretched out, resting on an elbow, so they could whisper, as he lay close to her. "I have some questions. Who's Franz?"

"Franz Berger. He's a cruel man, a killer, I'm sure, and commands the toughs hired."

"He tried to kill me on the Choctaw Plains while I was coming in answer to your letter. Did you tell anyone you'd sent for me?"

33

"No. My husband violently opposed it. So, I spoke to General Crook and he promised to have a letter waiting for you at Fort Fetterman but I'd given up hope of your coming, it's been so long. And somehow, my husband learned of the letter. He actually beat me with his fists, and won't let me leave the house without an escort. I'm a prisoner here."

"Why is he so much against my trying to find your son?"

"I can't tell you that. He and Franz are up to something in Fort Smith. It has to do with the Indian Territory, but I don't know just what it is. Adolf has powerful connections in Washington."

"You believe your boy was carried off by Indians?"

"I think he wanted to go there, and I hope he's still alive."

"Indians are very kind to children, Madame Froleiks. They won't harm him, though sometimes they'll kill white captives if the Army is so close they may be caught with them. There are quite a few white women and both white boys and girls hidden in the depths of the Nations. Only another Indian could hope to rescue them. If he's there, I believe I can find him and bring him back to you."

Impulsively, she seized him and kissed his cheek in a gesture of excited affection. Men feared Jim Sundance, but many women were drawn to him as a steel filing is to a powerful magnet.

"Tell me," he asked, "your first husband, Roland's father, was killed by the Germans in the Franco-Prussian War. Yet—you married Froleiks."

"I left France with my boy, shortly after the war, and came to the United States. I met Adolf in the

34

East; he was very handsome, and can be charming—when he so wishes. He insisted he was a Swiss German, not a Prussian. But too late, I realized he'd lied to me. He pays me little attention now; he has other women, but a French wife understands this. All men are polygamous, at least when they're virile and young enough. When they grow old, then they become monogamists." She shrugged.

"You have a picture of your Roland?"

"Yes. I have the large photograph, though I'd hate to part with that. I can give you a smaller one."

"Please do."

Without any false modesty, she threw off the covers and rose. She went to her bureau, and brought out a small photograph of the lad in the large frame, handing it to him, and looking appealingly into his eyes. "Please bring back my son to me, Mr. Sundance."

"I will if I can."

"I have some money. I can give you some now, and I'll have more later, when we meet again."

She stood close to him, looking up, studying the strong, grim face.

It was impossible to hide what he felt, as he caught her perfume, and he could see her many charms. His black eyes burned with the fire of his desire, and then she reached up and gently stroked his bronzed cheek. The touch of her fingers was like a caress.

"If you bring my son back to me," she said huskily, "I'll give you, not only money, but myself. I feel you admire me, and I no longer have the slightest affection for Adolf. He is ruthless, and cruel to me, my son hates him, and fears him. You do like me, don't you, Sundance?"

"I do."

He could no longer resist her spell. He swept her up, with a rough male clasp, and pressed a kiss on her full red lips. She responded, and he felt the vibrant desire flowing between a strong male and a warm, willing female, Nature's oldest urge.

She seemed more like an Indian woman, or like Barbara and Maggie, who had willingly given themselves to him, with the deepest, fondest passion.

And he knew he didn't need to restore her son to her to take the most desirable part of his reward; he could have her now, put her down and enjoy her, as she'd enjoy his manly attentions. He ran his hands over her soft hips, her bosoms.

Jim Sundance usually demanded a written contract in his dealings with white men. They were too likely to write him off as just another redskin, to be cheated and cast aside on the dump heap, once he'd served them.

But he forgot this; he felt that Simone would never go back on a promise.

Yes, Simone was responding, and he felt her trembling in his strong arms. She could read the desire in his flaming eyes, could feel how much he needed her as he crushed her close to his lean, muscular body.

She sighed deeply and murmured, "You—you are wonderful, Sundance, wonderful!"

She was his, all he need do was claim her.

It required all the steel resolution he could muster to resist the lovely woman who was offering herself to him.

But much as he wished, Jim Sundance knew this

was no time to dally. Soon, Franz would round up some of his gunhands, and fetch them back for the manhunt. They'd have an arsenal of weapons, bull's-eye lanterns with which to sweep every section of the grounds.

And with sentries posted, Sundance would have a hard fight to get clear, if he wasn't wounded or killed.

He put Simone down, holding her before him and searching her pretty face. "Then you don't know why your husband is so determined to keep me away from here. Or just why he and Berger have come to Fort Smith?"

"As I told you, I have no clear idea, although I believe they are interested, somehow, in the Indian Territory."

It was a shame he'd had to lay out the gunny who'd been waiting outside for Franz Berger, which had set off the alarm. Franz mightn't be sure Sundance had been there but they knew Simone had sent for him through Three Stars, as General George Crook was called by the Indians. And Berger had tangled with Sundance on the Choctaw Plains.

"I must go at once," he said. "I'll find your son and fetch him back to you if it's possible. I have the photograph you gave me—"

He broke off. He listened, warning her with an upraised hand to be silent. His keen ears had caught the whinny of a horse at the front of the big house. Another animal answered, and he heard the dull thud of hooves. A man, it sounded like Franz Berger, was singing out orders in a sharp voice.

"Quick," he warned. "Get back into bed. If your husband questions you, say you were asleep, and

37

that you saw nobody."

She nodded, looked alarmed. With his catlike tread, he crossed, turned out the lamp, glided to the open window and slipped out, seizing the oak tree limb.

But he was only part way down when he saw a dark figure framed against the street lanterns. A man was hurrying around the house, toward the wing where Sundance perched in the tree. He froze to the trunk, hoping the sentry would pass by.

His cartridge belt, the heavy Navy Colt in the holster, was within reach of his long arm, but for the time being, he let it hang there. The metal cartridges might clink and draw the guard's attention.

The sentry was almost to the tree when he stopped. He was looking up, and maybe he'd noticed when Sundance had turned off Simone's lamp. The man suddenly opened the slide of a bull's-eye lantern, and the beam swept slowly along the second-story windows of Simone's bedroom.

Sundance was still on the side nearer the building, and he never moved a muscle as he pressed to the rough bark. The stabbing beam passed by. Then the slide was closed.

A downstairs window sent a mellow light shaft into the yard. Sundance's eyes had adjusted so he could see the gunhand's Stetson, the paler oval of the face under the hat as he kept looking up. The faint light glinted on the burnished fat barrels of the weapon the man carried at the ready under his right arm. They were short barrels, a shotgun sawed off so the murderous thing could be used as a handgun.

It was one of the most dangerous killing machines known at close range, Sundance was well aware of that. Loaded with buck, it could blow a man in half with a single horrible blast, and Sundance had seen it happen more than once in his long, checkered career as an ace fighting man.

The gunny stood under the spreading oak; he seemed unsure of what his next move should be, whether to check further at this spot or to go on.

Jim Sundance tensed, watching for a slight chance to drop on his prey, like a cougar making ready to attack an animal below.

Then he heard Franz Berger's harsh voice, calling to his aide from the front:

"You see anything down that way, George?"

George swung to face the street, calling, "Nothin' yet, Chief."

"Check for footprints," ordered Berger. "Then post yourself where you are."

George again opened the lantern slide, directing it on the ground under the big tree. There were cast-off, dry leaves, and also brown acorns beneath the oak, and Sundance, any good tracker, would instantly have seen that some of the acorns were pressed into the earth when somebody had trod on them.

Sundance figured that this was his last, his only chance. He snatched his gunbelt and threw it over his left shoulder. Bowie knife gripped to stab rather than slice the belly as he would in a knife duel, he launched himself and landed on George's back.

The sharp point of the Bowie plunged unerringly into the soft area just above the collarbone, stabbing deep, and blood spurted as the blade severed the carotid artery. Sundance felt the warm fluid splatter his cheek; it had been imperative that he silence

George so he might get away from there.

As he'd landed on George, the gunhand had crumpled up. He was dead as he hit the ground, Sundance twisting the Bowie as he withdrew it; it made a soft, unpleasant "plop" as he yanked it free.

But George's shotgun had been on full cock, his finger on the front trigger, filed to a sensitive point so it would discharge instantly. Either reflex action or the hard jolt as he fell caused the man's finger to work convulsively.

The shotgun flamed lead, fire and smoke, and the full charge of buck ripped up a chunk of turf a yard away. The weapon then flew from George's relaxing hand.

The explosion sounded like a small cannon being touched off at a Fourth of July celebration. It deafened Sundance for a moment, his ears rang. And he knew what it meant. This would fetch Franz Berger and the whole passel of manhunters on him. They'd have more bull's-eye lanterns.

He would have to run the gantlet in an attempt to reach safety, and get clear of the house and grounds.

He heard Berger's furious voice bellowing commands. And as he started off, the bloody, wet Bowie knife in one hand, the Navy Colt jouncing against his ribs as he ran, several light beams stabbed at him.

"There he is!" thundered Berger. "Kill him!"

They opened fire as they sighted him in the crisscrossing beams.

Sundance, head down, ran as fast as he could.

And he knew that if he made it, he'd be lucky.

FOUR

Zigzagging as a man does when running the gantlet, Sundance headed for the board fence at the rear of Froleiks' property.

He heard a confused uproar of shouts behind him, shut off as a bullet shrieked close to his ear. He'd thrust the bloody Bowie knife into its sheath and drawn his Navy Colt, ready to fire. Two dark figures yelled as they saw him appear as he passed the back of the kitchen wing. "Here he is!" bellowed one.

Sundance fired immediately in their direction, hoping to rattle them as they raised their carbines. He was partially successful, for both ducked and swerved, but he felt a tearing, shocking sensation in his upper left arm and knew he'd been hit.

He grimly fought off the stunning effect and reached the fence. He went over it fast, as bullets slammed into the thick boards.

Dropping like a big cat, he caught his breath, could feel blood running down his left arm.

But he dared not even wait for the worst of the

shock to pass; head swimming, he loped toward a stable in the rear of the house on the adjoining street. There were lights in some windows, and a back door opened. A man with a pistol in one hand looked out, alarmed by the hubbub from Froleiks' place, called, "What's going on over there!"

"Stop him—stop that feller," yelled one of Berger's hands who had started across the fence on Sundance's trail. "He's a killer!"

But Jim Sundance had flitted past, and reaching the next street, turned toward the Arkansas.

He crossed over and trotted down the first driveway he came to, heading along the alley, with stables and barns across from the homes—there was usually such a service alley where the people kept their horses, feed for the animals, and vehicles.

The hue and cry was diminishing. They'd lost sight of him in the night. Blood kept dripping from his left arm, and he paused in the black shadow behind a hay barn to wrap his bandana around the arm, between the wound and shoulder, to slow the bleeding.

While they couldn't follow the trail of blood he left, in the night, when daylight came, expert trackers could pick it up. He pouched the Colt, and held his left arm crooked and pressed to his chest.

This checked the worst of the bleeding, and remaining drops soaked into his shirt; soon, it stopped altogether.

There were always people who kept on night lights, or who stayed up late, so plenty of places were illuminated. The section of the city where honky-tonks and such dives operated was some blocks away, toward the center.

He was very much worried about Simone Froleiks. She'd have to lie her way out of it, and perhaps her husband would believe her when she insisted she hadn't seen Sundance, that he must have been intercepted by Berger's gunhands before he could locate Simone and speak with her. It would sound logical, since it would be presumed that Sundance might have had trouble finding her bedroom. Also, they might think that Bernie challenging the interloper would have forced him to move most carefully . . .

It seemed much farther to the livery where he'd left Eagle than it had before he'd been wounded and run off, like a hare pursued by a pack of baying, ferocious hounds.

But at last he came near it, and reconnoitered carefully before moving in. There was a faint light in the front office, and the door was shut, but he looked in at a window and saw the Cherokee wrangler, Tall Littleman, dozing in a chair tilted back against the wall near the small office desk. A lantern, wick turned low, rested on the desk top.

He knew he could trust Tall Littleman, who was an Indian.

Sundance opened the latched front door from the road into the office. He did this with scarcely a sound, but Tall Littleman awoke instantly, with an Indian's alertness. The front legs of the chair hit the rough boards of the floor, his dark eyes opened and then he recognized the visitor.

"Sundance! You—you're wounded." Sundance's left shirt sleeve was soaked with blood.

"It's a flesh wound, Tall Littleman. Now, you must help me, and very quickly, as quickly as you

43

can. Get my bags and saddle my appaloosa. I must cross the river and hide myself in the Nations. Above all, remember you've never seen me."

Tall Littleman nodded; he was a willing ally. He hurried through a connecting door into the main stable, and Sundance heard him rummaging around, perhaps in some loft where he had stowed the parfleche bags.

On the desk, among other items, were several pencils and a pad of paper. Sundance sat down and began to write.

He composed a telegram to be sent to Barbara Colfax in Washington, D.C.:

Have our man check carefully on activities of Adolf Froleiks in regard to Indian Territory. When you have all facts, wire John Olliphant, Ft. Smith, Arkansas. Message to be held until called for by messenger.

Then he wrote a short message addressed to the Fort Smith telegraph operator: "Please deliver telegram to bearer." He signed this, "John Olliphant."

By the time he'd finished the two sheets, he heard the big front door of the livery being opened, and soon Tall Littleman appeared at the open street door, leading Eagle. The parfleche bags, the bedroll, the high-pronged saddle rode on the appaloosa's strong back; the Henry rifle, with its belt of ammunition, was in place.

Sundance stood up and went outside, touching Eagle, who was glad to see him. He would stand, now, wait for his human friend until Sundance was ready to ride.

Jim Sundance was aware that Indians were not permitted by law to possess strong liquor, either in

44

Fort Smith or in the Territory. White bootleggers would supply firewater for a price to the redskins, but when Judge Isaac Parker's deputy marshals caught up with them, the magistrate would deal severely with the miscreants, handing down sentences of five years or more in federal prison.

But Sundance had a small flask of whiskey in one of his bags and he dug it out and took it into the office. "I need a bucket of fresh water and a clean cloth," he told his young friend.

The Cherokee padded softly off in his moccasins. He soon came back with a pail of water and a cloth. Sundance removed his shirt, carefully, so the torn sleeve wouldn't stick to the drying wound. Tall Littleman was a real help; he examined the injury, and said, "It's not bad, a clean hole through the flesh."

Sundance handed him the flask of whiskey. "Now pour this into the rips in the flesh." He held his arm out straight, and Tall Littleman doused the wound; Sundance bent over to his right so the alcoholic fluid would flush the other side. It stung but Sundance showed not the slightest wince of pain.

"Do you know where the telegraph office is?" he asked.

"I know where it is though I've never been there."

"You must take this message to the telegraph office, and order it sent. Do it secretly, tell nobody, not even your employer. In two or three weeks, go back again and show this note. It's signed 'John Olliphant,' a name I've made up to hide my identity. You must conceal the reply when it comes, and hold it for me until I come again. Do you live in Tahlequah?"

"No, I sleep in a stable loft here when I'm not on

duty. But my parents and many relatives are there, and when I have a day off, I ride to see them."

Sundance's shirt sleeve had dried enough; he wiped it as clean as he could, and Tall Littleman expertly bandaged the flesh wound in his arm. Sundance took a short swallow of the whiskey, but only to brace himself. He could drink little hard liquor, and was most careful not to overimbibe. His Indian strain would not let him; it rebelled against alcohol and would turn him into a temporary madman, as it did with many savage peoples.

Now he fixed a smoke. Tall Littleman opened a drawer and brought forth a cash box. He took out the money Sundance had left to pay for Eagle's board and care for a week and held it out.

"You owe only one grain feed and part of a day."

"Tall Littleman, you must keep all that, for you'll have to pay for the long telegram. Also, you must not tell your boss that I have been here at all. If you wish, you can say a customer bought a nosebag of oats for his horse and leave that in the cash box."

Sundance then pressed more money on Tall Littleman, telling him he wanted to be certain that there would be plenty to pay for the telegram, and also to reward him for his time and cooperation.

"You don't need to pay me to help you, Sundance. It's an honor," insisted Tall Littleman.

But as Sundance so ordered, he pocketed the money.

"I'll cross the Arkansas and sleep in the hills," said Sundance. "I may head first to Tahlequah. Who is your Principal Chief now, Tall Littleman?"

The wrangler gave him the name in Cherokee; translated, it meant, Our Wise One.

When he was sure that Tall Littleman had all his instructions memorized, Sundance stepped out and swung into the high-pronged saddle. Behind rode the parfleche bags, on the great appaloosa's rump; he had his bedroll and trail rations. He was weary, and must soon rest, but first he had to cross the river and put as much distance as he could between himself and Fort Smith. Froleiks and Berger would already be spreading the alarm throughout the town.

He thought again of Simone, and prayed Froleiks wouldn't hurt her, would swallow the story she told him.

The river ran low; the waters were turgid; waste from the city flowed into it from many homes, from a large brewery and new plants set up in the burgeoning city. Garrison Avenue, near the center, was still brightly lit; the street ended at the river but there was a ferry plying back and forth across the stream.

He could see well enough to ride by, though there was no moon, and he used the stars to guide his general course. First, he must get out of town, for Berger would spread a general alarm. By morning, large rewards would be posted for Sundance, dead or alive. The blood-money hunters would take off like so many hounds on his trail. They would guess he had crossed the river and plunged into the Nations.

This was obvious to the keen mind of the man on the appaloosa stallion.

He saw the sheen of the water and put Eagle down the muddy bank, holding his rifle above his head so as not to wet it.

And then the horse found footing on the opposite shore, slowly climbed the bank, water dripping off his satiny hide.

There were cabins over here, near the river, and he avoided these. It was slow going in the darkness, but he pressed on at the best speed possible. As he came out on a winding dirt road, he could see the black shapes of the Cookson Hills rising in the sky before him.

Two hours later, he reached the shores of a large lake, and dismounted. Carefully, he located a spot where he could throw his roll. He unsaddled, and turned Eagle loose, for the stallion wouldn't stray far from him. The animal would also warn him if anyone was approaching as he slept.

Both the man and the horse drank from the clear water. Sundance wasn't hungry; he'd had a large supper before he'd gone to contact Simone Froleiks. He fixed a cigarette by sense of touch, and found it relaxing after his ordeal. Head on saddle, cushioned by a bed of thick spruce needles, blanket over him, Sundance was almost immediately asleep.

He slept soundly, rousing in the first gray of the dawn. Eagle was grazing nearby, close to the lake shore. This country abounded with small and large lakes, with streams; now he could make out the shapes of the Cooksons, which were really small mountains.

Sundance shed his clothes. He was careful not to disturb the bandaged arm; it stung but the wound was apparently healing well. His superb physical condition, the alcohol in the whiskey preventing possible infection, helped in this natural process.

Naked, he went to the lake and waded in. He washed carefully, but kept his upper left arm and the bandage out of the water. The bath was refreshing. He rolled a smoke, then found hardtack and jerky, which, washed down with lake water, allayed the pangs of hunger.

Now he began to unpack his parfleche bags. In one, he carried his short but powerful bow of juniper wood lashed with sinews and tipped with buffalo horn. In the panther skin quiver were the special arrows, which had flinthead points. He also found his ax, or tomahawk, as the white men called the hatchet. He checked all his weapons, the Colt Navy revolver, with its yellowed ivory butt, the repeating Henry rifle, making sure the firearms were loaded and clean, ready to use. He honed his Bowie knife, which had a 14-inch blade with a special hilt for fighting, crafted in New Orleans. His holster and saddle had been made by the expert craftsmen in Santa Fe.

Next, he opened the longer parfleche bag and carefully drew forth his Cheyenne war bonnet, elegant with beadwork. The eagle feathers had ermine tufts suspended from them, each feather denoting a brave deed.

Jagged, healed scars showed on both of his breasts, for he was a member of the Dog Soldier Society of the Cheyenne. In the Sun Dance, rawhide thongs were skewered through the tendons, and buffalo skulls were attached to the lower ends, long thongs fastened to the top of a high pole. The brave had to dance around until the breast thongs ripped through the tendons. The Sun Dance not only proved his courage and ability to withstand pain, but it also had religious significance.

He had a shield made of juniper wood, with a buffalo neck hide cover that would stop a revolver or light rifle bullet, though heavier weapons would penetrate it.

His treasures, of which he was quietly proud, were undamaged.

He thought of his mother, Shining Woman, the beautiful chief's daughter, his father's mate. Nick Sundance and his wife had traveled everywhere with their son, teaching him white man's and Indian's lore. And then—when Jim wasn't with them, bandits had murdered and robbed his parents. The son had hunted the six killers down, killed and scalped them, three whites, three Indians, and kept the dried scalps as trophies, attached to his war bonnet . . .

He stowed the bonnet but kept his bow and quiver. He rolled up his white man's clothing and stuffed it in a saddlebag. Now, he would become all Indian again. He carried the necessary equipment with him, fastened on his loincloth. He painted his face and torso with the proper colored streaks, showing his tribe and his standing. Other Indians would recognize the markings, and so would white men versed in identifying the various tribes. He dug out a broad rattlesnake-skin headband; it covered some, though not all, of his flaxen hair. And he had a wide leather belt he buckled about his waist; this would hold his Bowie sheath, and he could thrust his Navy Colt into it. He'd let the cartridge belt and revolver holster ride in a handy position on the saddlehorn, with the ammunition belt for the Henry rifle.

A man in white man's garb would attract attention in the Nations, but an Indian would not be such an object of curiosity. He might slip by Judge Parker's deputy patrols, and also the blood-money hunters who would already be swarming across to win the rewards he knew would be posted by Froelicks and Berger for his capture, dead or alive. Such men were like vultures, the avid blood-money toughs, eager for a victim. Many were no better than the usual killers and thieves they captured and often shot down from ambush, if the reward poster said "Dead or Alive."

He saddled Eagle, and arranged his parfleche bags, his bedroll and weapons. He slipped the bowstring of the short bow over his left shoulder, past the bandage; the arm was stiff, but he knew it was healing. His quiver was close to one side, so he could seize and nock an arrow in a flash, sending it on its silent but deadly mission. It had the advantage that it made no sound, as a gun would when fired.

The sun was coming up over Fort Smith, to the east, when he was ready to move on. He would first visit Tahlequah and inquire there for possible news of Roland. Swinging a long leg over the high-pronged saddle, he found a deer trail leading around the lake in the approximate direction he wished to go.

The sun began warming the mountain air, fresh and invigorating. For a time, Sundance rode in comparative safety, screened by the growth around the lake. He reached the western shore of the lake, and paused to check, for he would have to cross an open meadow. All round were hilltops, looking down in the valley in which he moved. Possible observers on the heights would see him, if they were on the alert.

He quickened the appaloosa's pace, Eagle's legs swishing through kneehigh grasses. There was a wooded slope ahead, about a quarter of a mile, and he made for this, where he would again be hidden from spying eyes.

He was relieved as he reached a grove of young ash and hickory trees; he recognized others, a scattering of gum and oaks. Sundance knew many trees, but it would have taken a botanist to identify all the magnificent growth of the Indian Nations.

Yes, he mused, a lovely land, with plenty of game and fish, roots and berries on which red men could subsist—if only they could hold onto it, hold it from the grasping, avid white eyes!

Suddenly, Sundance alerted, and he felt the appaloosa's handsome hide ripple, warning that he'd scented other horses or something unusual. Sundance's nostrils flared; a puff of the rising morning breeze brought him a scent of wood smoke.

The short bow snagged on the left arm bandage, but he quickly cleared it, and nocked an arrow from the panther-hide quiver into the string.

Then a friendly voice said to him in English, "Howdy, John. Nice mornin', ain't it?"

Behind a thick bole of a spruce slouched a man who needed a shave; he was a white, in dirty clothes, and it was plain it was a long time since he'd bothered to wash himself. Sundance could smell the sweaty body odor. He held a Winchester repeating carbine, a modern repeating weapon which looked well-cared for. But it was under his arm and pointed at the ground. The man gave him a wide grin, somewhat crooked due to a chaw of tobacco in one leathery cheek, and a front tooth was missing. "Light and set, John," invited the stranger. "Got coffee heatin' and I'll cook some bacon, too. Don't you speak English?"

Sundance knew he could kill the other man with an arrow before the fellow could raise and fire the carbine. But he never hunted trouble, and killed only when it was necessary, possibly for revenge, as with the murderers of his parents, the bandidos who'd raided their camp.

He decided to play dumb. He shook his head, and the stranger asked, "Ain't you a Cherokee?"

Sundance tried sign language but the man looked puzzled. Sundance watched, keeping a dull look on his face as the camper pointed off to a small clearing on the right. A fire burned there, and now Sundance caught the appetizing odor of coffee boiling. A cup would go well and so would some crisp strips of bacon—

Then Eagle snorted; the stallion whinnied, he'd scented a mare not far off—a mare? Three answered the stallion's call.

As Sundance immediately grew suspicious, aiming to get out of there, a hard voice behind him said, "Raise your hands and slide off, Injun, or we'll riddle you!"

The grin faded from the first man's face and up came the carbine.

FIVE

A second threatening voice, from the other side, behind Sundance, snapped, "Hustle, get down, John."

Three of them, at least, and he could see only the one in front of him. If he somehow managed to throw himself off the appaloosa and roll behind a tree, try to fight it out, they could kill Eagle. The odds were impossible.

Sundance slowly put his hands up, over his head; it hurt to stretch the left one, with the bandaged wound, but he showed no sign of pain. Hands up, he slid from the saddle. "Drop that bow, son," advised one of the still unseen men, and Sundance obeyed, standing with hands raised.

He glanced around, carefully. A man with a sixshooter leveled at him, the hammer spur back under a long thumb, was perched in a tree limb. There was another one on the far side of a big spruce, with a double-barreled shotgun on him.

If they were blood-money hunters, why hadn't

they shot him?

Nobody remembered that "John" wasn't supposed to understand English; they'd been too busy capturing him, and then, pointed guns spoke a language all men understood.

The shotgunner stepped into sight, keeping the murderous black eyes steady on the captive. He was older than the others, his beard and shaggy hair salted with gray. The third jumped down from his perch and joined the party, all three covering Sundance.

They kept a wary distance from him and showed they knew what they were doing.

"Hey, Pop," exclaimed the first, who'd lured Sundance into the trap, "look at that appaloosa! Bet he's worth a thousand."

Pop cleared a rheumy throat. "Two," he said dispassionately. "But right now I wouldn't take a million for him, Cappy."

"I claim him, Pop," said the third. "I spotted him first, when the Injun was crossin' that meadow."

"No, Harry, I'll keep him. And we got to skedaddle out of here fast as we can go. Them cussed deputy marshals missed us by inches yesterday, and when Esmeralda went lame, it looked like we was done for. But the devil saved our necks this time. We'll leave Esmeralda, fair trade with the Injun. She's old, too."

"So're you," growled Harry, angry at being refused Eagle.

"Not that old, Harry." There was a dangerous ring to Pop's voice. Sundance figured that, although he wasn't old enough to be the other pair's father, he was the leader.

Now he grew convinced they were not blood-money hunters. They must be outlaws, being hotly pursued by a party of Judge Parker's deputy federal marshals, and one of their horses, a mare named Esmeralda, had gone lame as they desperately sought escape.

Pop took another look at Sundance. "Huh, that's funny," he said. "He looks like a sure-enough Injun, but he's got light hair! Never seen that before. Could be he's a breed or maybe part albino. But that makes no nevermind right now. Pack the gear, Cappy, and we'll take off. No time to waste, I can almost feel them deputies breathin' down my neck."

"Let's kill this redskin," suggested Harry.

"No," said Pop. "Trouble with you, Harry, you're a fool, all you want to do is empty redeye bottles and consort with do-si-do girls. The Indians in the Territory don't bother us, as long as we don't bother them. You kill one, you'll have his whole tribe on your trail. This one looks like a Cheyenne, at least his markins' say so. I've seen plenty of 'em around Fort Sill and elsewhere. Yeah, you want to kill, only at the wrong time! Instead of just layin' out that bank clerk in Van Buren, you should've stuck your knife in his heart. Then he couldn't 've described us to the police and set the marshals on our trail so quick."

Harry might be a fool, but Sundance could see that Pop wasn't. As he spoke, the pale-blue, washed-out eyes under the shaggy brows were alert, never wavering off the captive. The shotgun was aimed dead center on Sundance, and Pop's finger was on the trigger of the cocked weapon. He couldn't miss at such close range.

Carefully, keeping his hands up, Sundance squatted down. His face was a set, inscrutable mask. He maintained the stupid look and manner; they still believed he was just another Indian, or maybe a breed.

"Fetch up the horse, Harry," ordered Pop. "Move, boy. Them deputies would pick up our trail at dawn and they ain't far off. They know we got a lame horse, they can read it in our sign. Pronto, throw on our packs and check the cinches."

Harry shrugged and slid his Colt revolver into the holster.

Sundance waited; he'd dropped his bow and it lay just beyond his reach.

Soon Harry reappeared, leading three horses from a grove off to the left. There was a lithe, black critter, and a sturdy mare. The third was past her prime, and limped badly, favoring her right foreleg. Her head was down, and her spirit seemed gone. That must be Esmeralda, whom Pop would trade for the magnificent Eagle.

Sundance waited. He knew what was going to happen, and that might offer him his chance.

Maybe they wouldn't kill him. But the federal marshals weren't far away, and hot on the trail. On a lame mount, Sundance would have little or no chance of escape. The word would quickly spread that Sundance was wanted for murder. The officers would see his flaxen hair, though he'd chopped some of it off. The Indian getup wouldn't fool such men. Adolf Froleiks and Franz Berger would have started the chase, big rewards were posted for the capture of an Indian with hair the color of new wheat. Even if the marshals pursuing Pop and his boys hadn't yet heard about Sundance, they'd hold him because he'd be riding Esmeralda, and without a horse, he didn't think he'd get far.

"Ready, Pop," announced Cappy.

Pop started backing toward Eagle. He never took his eyes off the squatted Sundance. "Draw your hogleg and shoot him if he moves, Harry," ordered Pop. "When I get aboard, I'll cover him while you boys mount. We take off, and fast."

Pop shifted the shotgun to his left hand. He held it like a big pistol. He reached for Eagle's bridle and the appaloosa gave the hand a vicious bite. Blood spurted from it, and Pop swore.

"Help me hold this animal, Cappy," he cried. "This animal is nasty. When I get the saddle, I'll give him a good taste of the quirt and spurs so he'll learn to behave."

Cappy hustled over and skillfully caught a short hold on Eagle's rein so the appaloosa hadn't enough scope to bite.

Eagle reared, lifting Cappy clear off the ground, whirling, so the man was flung under him, losing his grip. The big stallion came down with all his weight on the sprawled man, with Cappy under him. Forelegs dropped, Eagle kicked.

There was a sickening "plop" as the appaloosa's hoof connected with Pop's head and the skull smashed like an eggshell. The shotgun blasted, its load burrowing in the earth.

Sundance had known exactly what Eagle would do. The horse would permit nobody to touch him unless Sundance told him to do so.

Harry panicked as he saw Cappy crushed and senseless, Pop's brains scattered all over everything.

He let out a hoarse shout of alarm, and turned his revolver on Eagle to shoot him down.

Sundance fell forward, snatching his Bowie knife from its sheath.

The 14-inch Bowie flew from Sundance's expert, unerring hand. The sharp point tore into Harry's soft belly, ripping the intestines. Harry screamed in agony, and his Colt exploded, the slug flying over Eagle into the trees.

Now Sundance snatched up his bow, nocked an arrow into the string, and let fly. The flint head buried itself in Harry's heart and the man went down.

He stepped over to check. Harry and Pop were very dead, and Cappy couldn't draw any breath into his crushed lungs; he was unconscious, and he'd soon expire. Sundance retrieved his arrow from Harry's body, and cleaned it on the man's shirt, returning it to the quiver. They were perfect arrows, difficult to come by and replace.

He unsaddled the three horses and let them loose to graze and water as they pleased. The three who'd tried to rob him of the appaloosa had nothing else he wanted; soon, the marshals would come along and find their job done for them. They wouldn't have to shoot it out with the trio and take them back to Judge Parker's court for trial. The hanging machine standing outside the building eventually would have had three more customers.

Sundance figured he'd done the deputies a big favor.

He dare not tarry, for the posse, according to what Pop had said, were too close for wasting any time.

He checked Eagle's cinches, the bags and his gear;

all seemed well. He mounted and rode off, without a backward glance.

The roar of Pop's shotgun, the sharp report of Harry's heavy Colt's .45 caliber revolver, would carry some distance on the wind, which was from the west. The deputy marshals, hot on the outlaws' trail, might very well have heard the sounds.

Sundance pulled up half a mile from the spot where he'd had the fracas. He climbed a tall spruce, and from this height, could see back toward the meadow where he'd crossed and been seen by the three who'd captured him.

A party of riders, six of them, came at a swift pace toward the place where Sundance had been nailed. Half a mile behind them was a closed wagon drawn by two big mules. He knew that often the deputies out of Fort Smith would make protracted stays in the Nations, and the wagon carried supplies and also provided a safe spot in which to iron captives until the officers were ready to run them back to the "hole" in Fort Smith, a large and dreaded lockup in the basement of the main courthouse.

The jail was dank; the prisoners were crowded in, with often only much and water to eat. The sanitary facilities consisted of a few buckets which were emptied once a day. Imprisonment in the hole was feared almost as much as the large hanging machine in the yard outside, with armed guards ready to shoot down any possible escapees.

He descended the spruce as fast as he could, and rode on toward Tahlequah. But he had decided on one thing; he would not again cross open spaces during daylight, not after the pleasure of meeting Pop, Cappy and Harry.

The marshals would soon come upon the dead he had left behind for them. They would also pick up the tracks of a fourth horse, Eagle. And there was a good chance at least some of them would follow him.

Eagle scented water, and Sundance let him have his head. The appaloosa wound through the woods to a creek, lowered his muzzle and drank. Sundance drank, too, and washed his hands and face.

Now he remounted and rode along the other side of the stream for half a mile. The bottom was gravel and his tracks would be hidden. It was an old dodge, and no doubt the deputies were as familiar with it as Sundance was, but it would delay pursuit for a time.

He left the creek just below a small waterfall, breasting through thick brush. A muskrat scurried off the bank, dove into the creek and disappeared into the underwater connection into its burrow. The bushes snapped to behind him and he came out on a faint deer trail, where animals came down to drink.

In time, the deputy marshals, if they wanted him enough, would cast up and down the banks and eventually discover the spot where he had ridden out of the stream. But he would gain valuable hours. The officers would come upon the dead outlaws they had been after; they would find signs of the fight, and note Eagle's hoofprints. Sundance didn't believe that, as yet, this party of manhunters would guess who had done their job so efficiently for them. They'd be very curious, as well as mystified; an honest man who'd defended himself against Pop, Cappy and Harry wouldn't have fled at their approach. On the other hand, it was unlikely they'd have let Sundance ride on. They'd have first asked, then insisted he return to Fort Smith with them.

And then Berger and Froleiks would have him, Sundance was wanted for murder in the city. The party might meet other officers and trackers hunting for Sundance and he would be hopelessly nailed. To run for it was his only choice.

Blackbirds and other winged critters flew off as the big horse moved on, mainly northwest. Sundance was heading for Tahlequah, the center of the Cherokee Nation.

A remarkable tribe, the Cherokees. They had lived in southern Georgia and Tennessee, and had even been friends of the white men who invaded the new continent. The Cherokees were the only tribe which had never warred with the whites; when President Andrew Jackson had ordered them to remove themselves west of the Mississippi, they had obeyed. They were the only Indian tribe which had a written alphabet; others passed on tribal history from father to son, generation after generation. Young Senator Sam Houston, after an unfortunate first marriage, had suddenly given up his high position, everything he had, and gone to live with the Cherokees. Houston had married a Cherokee girl, according to their custom, and lived with his red friends for five years.

Houston had taken to drink; he'd become a sodden, helpless man. cared for by his benefactors. Then he'd pulled himself together, and returned to see Andrew Jackson; he was a protegé of the great President, a favorite with Jackson.

And Jackson had sent him on a secret mission into vast Texas, first Spanish, then Mexican after the revolution. The Texans had revolted against oppressive measures taken by Santa Anna, the powerful Mexican dictator. The Mexican armies, commanded personally by Santa Anna, had swept ruthlessly on; they'd attacked and reduced the Alamo, no quarter shown when the defenders refused to surrender. Bowie, Crockett and Travis had died with their handful of men . . .

Houston had retreated, retreated, retreated; but at Buffalo Bayou, he'd caught Santa Anna napping and had won an incredible victory, capturing Santa Anna himself.

For two terms, Houston had served as President of the Texas Republic; then President M.B. Lamar had driven the Indians, among them the peaceful Cherokees, from Texas soil. The remnants of the Cherokees who'd settled in Texas had to march in the dead of an icy winter, "The Trail of Tears," many women, children and older Indians dying before they reached their brothers at Tahlequah in the Indian Territory. An unhappy tale.

After the close call with Pop, Harry and Cappy, Sundance determined not to show himself out in the open during daylight. Rising mountains ahead, some with bare flanks, forced him to detour for a good many miles in order to skirt the heights. He spent the night in the woods, after riding as far as possible.

He killed a small fawn in the morning, using his bow and arrow, bled it, skinned it, and enjoyed a substantial meal of venison. He again slept in the forests, and too wary to ride straight into Tahlequah, he made a long detour so as to come in from the northwest.

He hid the appaloosa well back in the woods, and on foot approached to scout the settlement. The day was well along as he crouched in the bush, studying the busy village. Squaws were at work, older men sat in the shade, smoking and talking of former glories. Younger braves were no doubt out hunting meat. Children played with wooden knives and small bows and arrows, or swung on plaited vine swings. There were dogs lying around, but he was downwind, and they didn't scent him or give any alarm.

Horses were held nearby by older lads, herd guards.

Suddenly the dogs alerted, and sprang up, baying, but they weren't barking at Sundance. They were facing the southeast, the road leading to the Arkansas and Fort Smith.

Two whites rode in. They carried carbines and revolvers, and Sundance saw the deputy marshal badges glinting on their vests.

The dogs were called off, stones thrown at them by the boys, and the officers were greeted and invited to dismount by a couple of the Cherokee men.

Sundance lay, without moving a muscle, watching.

After a time, as the marshals' horses were led off to water and be seen to, a brave went to a larger lodge in the center of the village. Soon an elderly man came out; his hair was white, his face lined with the wrinkles of age, of wisdom. It was Our Wise One, the Principal Chief. With great dignity, the Chief welcomed the visitors, and invited them to eat and drink, make themselves at home.

Sundance was glad he hadn't yet visited the Cherokees, for they could honestly say they had not seen him. He didn't believe the pair came from the party who'd been after Pop, Cappy and Harry; they must be fresh from Fort Smith, hunting for the Indian with hair the color of new wheat, Jim Sundance, wanted for the murder of George, Berger's bullyboy whom Sundance had killed under Simone's windows . . .

The deputies drank, ate and rested, chatting with the Chief and a couple of older men. They remained at Tahlequah until the afternoon heat abated, their horses had been rested, fed and watered, then they took their leave and rode off, heading southwest through the Nations. Chances were they'd try the Osages next, then on, inquiring for news of the fugitive at the headquarters of one tribe after another. Sundance saw them leave a couple of circulars with Our Wise One, no doubt offering the large rewards posted for the capture of Sundance.

Sundance napped for a time, never really asleep, but relaxing and reviving his power. He waited until the sun was well down and the squaws had begun to prepare the evening meal at the outdoor hearths.

The Principal Chief had gone back into his lodge. His wife and daughters were busy at the fire, broiling meat, cooking sourdough biscuits, fixing dinner. He slipped silently, unobserved, to the back of the tepee and crawled in under the shelter; the sides were rolled up to permit circulation of air.

The Chief was sitting, his back to Sundance as he straightened to his full height. Our Wise One was smoking a long pipe, and he was deep in thought; he looked around as Sundance spoke to him softly, in Cherokee.

Sundance had met the Chief before, on visits to Tahlequah.

The Chief gravely regarded him, as Sundance squatted, Indian fashion, before him. He handed the pipe to his guest and Sundance puffed on it. The Chief welcomed him politely; the next thing he did was to pick up a circular and silently offer it to Sundance.

WANTED FOR MURDER: JIM SUNDANCE. $1000 REWARD, DEAD OR ALIVE!

There followed an excellent description of the fugitive. They not only accused Sundance of murdering a man named George, but for killing Murphy and Buck in the Choctaw Nation.

"You know," said Our Wise One, "we have our own Indian courts in the Nations, but when a white man is involved, then he must be turned over to the white authorities. I know you, Sundance, know you too well to believe you'd kill without good reasons."

Sundance briefly described what had happened on the Choctaw Plains, and then the dangerous escape from Adolf Froleiks' home in Fort Smith. He told the Chief how Three Stars had left word he was to help Simone Froleiks find her son.

Indians seldom showed any of their inner feelings, but Sundance was an Indian himself and he was watching the Chief's eyes. As he spoke of Roland, he did not miss the slight flicker which was as much surprise as Our Wise One might show.

"You've seen him, then," he said. He showed the photograph.

The Chief nodded. "Yes, he was here. We didn't

know who he was, he just said he wanted to be an Indian. He was hungry and tired, and we fed him, and our squaws petted him and were good to him. So were the Indian boys. Before long, the boy, who was very lively and clever, had shed his clothing, which was stained and torn by moving through the woods and brush, and dressed as one of us, wearing a pair of deerskin pants a squaw made him, feathers and paint. He played hard with our boys, they raced and waged mock battles.

"You know, we love all children, we never beat or hit them. I talked several times with this boy, and after two or three days, I thought he would be ready to tell me his name and would want to go home, but he said he would never go back, he hated his father, who whipped him often and anyway, he wasn't his real father."

"That would be Adolf Froleiks. Do you know who he is?"

The Chief shook his head.

"He is an evil man. I'm not sure what he's planning, but it will not help the Indians. I believe he is a dangerous threat to the Indian Nations. I'll find out exactly what he's up to. Now, go on, tell me what happened to Roland."

"Finally, I told him he must go back to his own people, that we would have to take him to Fort Smith next day. That night, he ran away. He took a little food, a knife, and he wore his Indian clothes and moccasins. When he was missed next morning, we thought he was just hiding in the forest and would come back, but he didn't and there was a hard rainstorm, so when our braves finally began to track him, it was impossible. And our men ran into a large Osage hunting party who accused them of trespassing on their grounds, and forced them to turn back. Next day, several men came here, inquiring for this boy. We dared not say we'd seen him and hadn't taken him back at once—you know how the whites are, they would have blamed us and made trouble for the Cherokees. After they'd gone, we wrapped the boy's clothing in a hide and buried it in the forest. I wouldn't tell this to any white man, but you are Sundance."

The Chief invited him to eat and spend the night, and Sundance enjoyed a hearty meal, after he'd brought in Eagle and unsaddled the appaloosa, leaving him to graze nearby. Sundance told the Chief of Tall Littleman, and how helpful the Cherokee had been to him. "Yes, he's a fine man. His parents live here in Tahlequah and he visits when he can and brings us presents."

Sundance slept in the Chief's tepee that night. He was up at dawn, found Eagle, saddled the appaloosa and secured his packs. He returned to eat breakfast with Our Wise One, smoking and talking for a time. Through the open flaps, he saw younger squaws starting out into the woods, with baskets. They would hunt for edible roots and berries, and Sundance was aware that 80% of Indian food was supplied by their squaws. The braves brought in meat and hides, protected the villages . . .

As Sundance was thanking the Chief for his hospitality, a lithe Cherokee brave trotted up to the lodge. The man had been running, and he reported, "Two whites are coming. They're not law officers. They are heavily armed and they look mean."

Sundance could guess what the pair must be:

blood-money wolves, hunting him down for the posted rewards.

He slipped away into the forest and led Eagle westward, away from the village. He hid himself and waited; several trails led from Tahlequah, and he meant to take one that would lead southwest. But first, he would see which way the manhunters went.

A pretty girl, a Cherokee maiden of perhaps fourteen or fifteen, whom he'd noticed in the village, came along the path. She wore soft deerskin, moccasins on her small feet, and she was carrying a basket which she was filling with roots and berries she found in the woods and in the small clearings.

Sundance kept quiet and let her pass. She disappeared around a bend in the trail, and then he heard hoofbeats coming from Tahlequah.

Two riders appeared, one ahead, the second close behind. They wore Colts, and they carried carbines and knives. Neither had shaved or washed for some time, and their red-rimmed eyes showed they were heavy drinkers. As the Cherokee brave had reported, they looked "mean". Sundance had seen plenty of such buzzards, who made a more or less precarious living hunting down fugitives; when the posters said "Dead or Alive," they usually brought back their prey filled with lead. It was easier and less dangerous to their own hides that way.

"Dog it, Ed, some of them Cherokee squaws look mighty juicy," said one, as they were passing the hidden, silent Sundance. "I could sure use a woman."

"Me, too, Maurie, me too—" The second broke off with a curse. "Hey, look over there, pickin' berries!"

Sundance guessed they must have sighted the

Cherokee girl he'd seen.

The two quickened pace, and went around the bend. Sundance rose, and trotted after them.

As he paused, hidden by a thick oak bole, he could see what went on. Ed and Maurie had both jumped down, dropping rein, and were approaching the girl, who suddenly turned, hearing them coming at her.

Sundance could see the fear in her dark eyes; she opened her mouth to scream for help, but one of the men leaped at her, clapping a hand over her mouth. She had a knife in her belt, but it was quickly snatched from her.

She was thrown down, her skirt raised, ripped aside. The first man mounted her, the second stood by, waiting his turn.

SIX

Sundance drew the Bowie knife.

A mounting fury burned within him. This was one of the things about white men which enraged him. They seemed to think an Indian female was no more important than an animal, to be used at their pleasure and cast aside without the slightest concern.

He stole closer, making no sound, his teeth bared.

The two were so intent on the pretty Cherokee girl, whom they were about to rape, that they were totally unaware of the lithe figure almost on them. The Indian girl was fighting with a wildcat's desperation. She raked her nails down the cheek of the man over her and nearly managed to squirm from under him.

"Grab the little bitch's arm and hold her down for me, Maurie," cried the fellow trying to overcome the girl. A thin trail of blood showed on his whiskered cheek.

Maurie had been impatiently awaiting his turn.

He knelt down, turning as he snatched at the Chero-kee girl's slim wrists to control her. The first man's sweat-stained Stetson had been knocked off during the struggle, exposing uncombed, longish and greasy black hair.

And as "Maurie" swung around so as to seize the girl's arms and hold her for his companion, he suddenly sighted the hatchet-faced Indian with the flaxen hair, Bowie knife poised, within striking distance. Sundance's long legs were bent, ready for the lunge.

Maurie let out a choked cry of fright and snatched at his holstered revolver.

"Ed!" he howled. "It's—it's *him*!"

They were the last words he ever spoke, for Sundance had launched himself at Maurie. The .45-caliber Colt was only part way out of the open, oiled holster as the sunlight in the small clearing flashed on the 14-inch steel blade of the Bowie knife.

Sundance struck with the deadly speed of a big rattlesnake. The long knife drove into Maurie's heart and he twisted it savagely, before ripping it from the gaping wound. Blood spurted out from a severed artery as the Bowie was jerked free, a sickening "plop" sounding as the knife was so suddenly pulled from Maurie's guts.

Maurie's mouth opened wide; his legs collapsed and he fell hard, kicking spasmodically, like a suddenly killed frog.

Ed reacted very fast. Still on his knees, he pulled his gun as he swung around and faced Sundance. The girl rolled free and came up in a crouch, trembling.

Ed was raising his pistol for the kill, as Sundance jumped past him, grasped the greasy black hair, and whipping him around, hit him as hard as he could in the nose. Ed's head snapped back and Sundance cut his throat from ear to ear.

The two blood-money hunters had unexpectedly found their quarry. Sundance checked them, though it wasn't necessary. Both were dead.

The Cherokee girl rose, straightened her clothing. She was shaking, fighting back tears which came into her large, dark eyes. Her rounded cheeks were flushed, but Sundance had saved her from rape.

"Thank you," she stammered, speaking Cherokee. "You—you are Sundance! You were at our village." She lowered her eyes, long lashes resting on her brown cheeks, with the modesty of an Indian maiden.

"Yes, I'm Sundance."

He took her by both arms, and in Cherokee, spoke to her: "Listen, most carefully. You will go back at once to your village and speak to Our Wise One, your Principal Chief. Tell him what happened and that Sundance came along in time to save you. You will also tell him that he needn't worry about these two chunks of carrion, that Sundance will guarantee they'll never be found. Do you understand all this?"

The girl looked into the stern, set face; her eyes softened. for Sundance had a magnetism which drew women to him, and the girl might not have objected so strenuously, if Sundance had desired her.

"I understand," she nodded. "I'll tell Our Wise One everything you've said."

"Tell nobody else. This is important. Don't let anyone know you've seen Sundance, particularly any white men who come to Tahlequah hunting for me. I've done nothing wrong, only defended myself, as I did just now in helping you, but the white men speak with lying tongues, the forked tongues of poisonous serpents."

She found her basket, which had flown off a few feet from where Maurie and Ed had thrown her down. She gave Sundance another look of the deepest reverence and gratitude, and ran off for the path back to Tahlequah.

Sundance wiped his Bowie knife clean on Maurie's torn shirt. The two saddled geldings the hunters had been riding were secured not far off, and he untied their reins and led them to the edge of the small clearing, fastening them to strong tree limbs. The animals didn't like the smell of the fresh blood; they snorted, and danced, but Sundance soon quieted them.

There were coiled lariats hanging from the hooks of both saddles, and Sundance pulled them off. He cut lengths to use as lead ropes, and then threw Maurie over the saddle of a gray. He made careful ties so the dead weight couldn't slide off. He put Ed over the second horse, a chestnut gelding, making sure of his knots. He thrust the men's revolvers into his belt; he didn't want them and would toss them into the first deep lake he came upon.

Now he fastened a lead rope from the gray's bridle ring to the horn of the chestnut's saddle, leaving enough slack so the animals wouldn't bump one another as they followed along. He wiped out what sign he could of the struggle in the grass, picking up Ed's hat, which had fallen off, and tying it to the chestnut gelding's saddlehorn by its leather chinstrap.

He called Eagle; the big appaloosa stallion came to him and Sundance tied the last length of lariat, which he'd saved, to the chestnut's bridle. Finally, he made a loop in the rope's end and drew it tight around the high horn of his own saddle.

Sundance had worked swiftly, with no wasted motions, knowing what he meant to do. With a last sweeping glance around the small clearing, he mounted Eagle and started back to the trail. The gray and the chestnut came along obediently as the ropes caught up, and they followed, Sundance moving at a slow pace.

At least, he thought, he'd saved the little Cherokee maiden. And there were two less blood-money hunters seeking his hide, though he knew there would be plenty more looking for him through the Nations.

He stayed on the trail for a time until he sighted one of the numerous jewel-like lakes studding the Territory. Getting down, he reconnoitered. The scene was peaceful, deserted, so he led the horses to the shore.

There were plenty of rocks strewn along the bank and more sticking from the shallows. He kicked off his moccasins and made a pile of suitable weights. Unfastening the ties, he pulled Ed off, and filled the man's clothing with stones. Satisfied with his work, he waded out and sank the body in several feet of water.

He repeated the process with Maurie. It should be some time before they rose to the surface, if they ever did. He tossed the pair's weapons into deep water.

Checking again to be sure he was not being watched, he stripped to the skin and washed himself carefully. A Cheyenne bathed daily, even in winter, when possible. Sundance was caked with dried blood from the kills, with dust and grit.

When he had cleaned himself, he dried off and put on his loincloth, moccasins and fastened his rattlesnake headband around his hair; he had cropped some off, but strands could be seen underneath the circlet.

He turned the gray and the chestnut loose. For a time they stood, watching him, unaware they were free. When they did, the horses would drink, and graze in nearby meadows. Both animals had blotched owner brands on them; probably they'd been stolen, maybe a long way from here, by the two rascals who'd been riding them. In time, they might find their way home to their real owners.

The wounded left arm hadn't bothered him much, and the bandage was soiled, wet from his swim, so he threw it away and left the wound uncovered. It was healing well; he'd watch it, but there was now very little chance of infection setting in. It was just another scar on his tough, muscled body, along with the Crow arrow scar on his cheek, received so long ago during a fight with the hereditary enemies of the Cheyenne.

He mounted Eagle, and started back to the trail west. He doubted if the two blood-hunters would ever be missed; such vultures traveled far and wide at their miserable trade, and had few if any connections. They were much different from officers of the law, who risked their lives attempting to arrest dangerous criminals.

The gray and the chestnut had drunk from the lake. As the appaloosa started away, they looked after Eagle, and then started to follow along. However, first the chestnut gelding noticed some fine bunch grass and paused to graze; then the gray stopped, looked around, and went back to help.

Hitting the trail, Sundance picked up speed. He'd lost a couple of hours, and the sun was well up; here and there, brilliant streamers broke through the forest and touched the path. He wished to put plenty of distance between himself and the spot where he'd taken care of Ed and Maurie.

There were mountains, hills, lakes all through this section of the beautiful Territory. Farther west, toward the Texas Panhandle, however, the country flattened out and there were thousands of acres of fine grazing land. Already, the Comanches and Kiowas were leasing grazing rights to white ranchers, who would fatten their cattle for market on the Indian grass. Yes, all in all, Indian Territory was a most valuable asset, of incalculable wealth. Probably there were mineral deposits not yet uncovered. The whites had seized *Pah Sapa*, the sacred Black Hills, from the Sioux and Cheyennes, because gold had been discovered there, and whites were in Montana, too.

It was a bitter thing, the ruthless seizure by the white men of the Indian lands. Every treaty, while sacredly observed by the redskins, had so far been broken whenever the *wasichun* discovered something they wanted on Indian ground.

The ferocious wars, the last ditch stand of the mighty Sioux and their blood brothers, the Cheyennes, had been brought on, first by seizure of the Black Hills of Dakota, and then brought to a head when gold had been discovered in Montana. The Indians had fought hard, to the best of their ability, but they had no weapons to combat the whites, who, as Red Cloud had once said, were as numerous as the leaves on the trees. The Battle of the Little Big Horn, when General George A. Custer and over two hundred of his 7th Cavalry had died, had been the end, really, for the northern tribes. Sitting Bull and Gall were still in Canada, and Sundance could only wage what seemed to be a losing battle as he fought to gain better terms for the redmen . . .

Sundance's keen nostrils widened; he'd felt Eagle ripple his hide, and the appaloosa had already told him there was smoke in the clean air. Sundance immediately veered off the winding trail, and dismounted.

He signalled to his horse to stand and wait until called or until Sundance returned, and Eagle would obey.

He stuck his pistol in his sash and pulled his Winchester carbine from the boot, checking the loads. He always wore his Bowie knife. Then he flitted silently through the forest aisles.

The smoke smell grew stronger and he drew closer and closer. Like a wraith, Sundance approached. There was a creek nearby, and he heard the stamp of horses' hooves, but they were standing, not on the move.

Now the sun was dropping in the western sky. He caught the odor of broiling meat in the smoke, and next he heard men's voices. They were Indians, and they were not looking for trouble, probably they'd gone into camp and were preparing the evening meal.

Sundance easily stole up to a point where he could

observe the gathering. There were about a dozen men gathered around the campfire, set in a small open space close to the stream. Their mustangs were grazing nearby, where they could drink when they wished.

The Indians were young men, bronzed torsos naked to the waist; they wore deerskin trousers with fringed, high moccasins, and their heads had been partly shaved, but a long, thick scalp lock was banded on top, like a stack of wheat.

Osages.

Sundance rose and called out a greeting, and the braves all jumped up. He knew some Osage talk, and they stood, watching, as the tall figure strode from the trees. The Indians were plainly hunters; they had rifles, and carried the usual knife, but the paint on their faces meant they were not on a raid.

One powerful Indian, with a barrel chest, stepped forward and greeted him. He was a few years older than the rest, about thirty perhaps, and was evidently leader of the party.

His black eyes suddenly took in the light hair on the visitor's head. "Sundance," he cried, and came forward with his hand stretched out, white-man fashion. Sundance heard the other braves murmuring his name, a magic name among the tribes.

The visitor was made very welcome, offered a buffalo hide to sit on, but first, Sundance told them he must bring up his horse. He trotted back and called Eagle, and the appaloosa followed him to the Osage camp. The Indians exclaimed over the big stallion's lines and sheer beauty. To an Indian, a horse was important.

The sub-chief of the Osages, who was called Buffalo Killer in English translation, offered Sundance a long pipe, and they squatted together, smoking for a time while the meat broiled. There were steaks cut from buffalo rump, and it smelled delicious as it sizzled on the sharpened sticks before the crackling fire. They also had some soda-biscuits, bought at a white man's store, some berries and pemmican.

Any Plains Indian much preferred bison meat above beef, which to the savage tasted rather bitter and unpleasant; it had not the sweetness of the buffalo flesh, and the steers given the Indians on the reservations were stringy, often diseased culls the whites didn't want.

When they had eaten, the guest being served the choicest pieces of the meat, they again smoked, squatted on their haunches.

Finally, Sundance brought up the subject of Roland; it wasn't considered polite to ask questions until a friendship had been cemented. The white eyes always wanted to talk business at once, without the usual ceremonial chat.

Buffalo Killer grinned.

"Yes, he was in our village. A white boy, dressed like an Indian. We knew he was a runaway. Some squaws out digging roots and picking berries met him. He was tired and his body was scratched; he was very hungry. They brought him to our camp, and the squaws petted him and fed him. You know, we all love children, no matter what color they may be.

"He was a brave boy and seemed unafraid of us. He was very lively, too, and made us laugh. He would wardance and pretend to scalp us. Some of us laughed till we rolled over, holding our bellies, so amused were we by his antics. Our boys played well with him, they wrestled and ran races and did tricks on their ponies, and the white boy was as good as any. As I've told you, he was lively and full of a brave spirit. We would have been glad to adopt him into our tribe, but we were afraid. You know how the white soldiers are, if they find a white among us, they blame the whole tribe and kill braves, squaws and children alike.

"The boy refused to tell us where he came from or his white man's name. Someone gave him a comic name in our language, which meant the Ferocious Flea! We didn't dare keep him, so our Principal Chief ordered us to take him with us through the Cherokee Strip, as I was to lead a party of hunters to bring in meat for the village. We were to turn south to Fort Sill on the way and order the boy to surrender himself to the soldiers at the Fort. He said he didn't want to go, but we made him, so he rode along on a pony we gave him as a present."

As with the Cherokees, Roland's capers had made a great hit with the Osages. The boy seemed to have worked out an act which immediately amused the savages, and he was making good use of it. He certainly wasn't stupid, thought Sundance; he could picture how Roland had kicked up and made the Indians laugh. It would disarm them, endear the boy to all.

Buffalo Hunter's party had swung off toward Fort Sill. They were fearful of being involved in Roland's disappearance, and only intended to make sure he rode his pony to the Fort. So they had camped some miles off; they were no longer in wooded country but in the flatter lands where white men leased grazing rights from the Comanches and Kiowas. There were herds of cattle around, but the Indians would not touch them, unless they were on a vengeful raid.

At dawn, they had put Roland on the pony given him and started him off on the trail to Fort Sill. The boy had promised he would go straight there.

The Osages had hurried on toward the hunting grounds. They'd avoided a party of Kiowas, who were unfriendly, and as everyone knew, the Kiowas were boiling mad because the white men had sent their great chief, Satanta, back to the Texas prison until he died.

Sundance nodded sadly. Satanta had been a close friend of his. The chief had been caught on a raid by the Army, away from the Indian Territory, arrested and sent to Huntsville, where he'd previously spent two years. Then he was pardoned, but on parole, told that if he was ever again arrested, he must return to the prison for the rest of his life.

When Satanta had returned to his people, he had become an embittered man. All he wished to do was kill white people, and he'd led many more raids, with the Comanches under Quanah, out to the Texas Panhandle and over the Llano Estacado, the Staked Plain. But finally, a cavalry patrol had caught up with him, and he had been returned to prison.

This had upset the Kiowas and they were acting like enraged hornets. The older chiefs counseled peace but the young braves demanded war, revenge.

Sundance, like all Indians, was aware that no savage could very long endure imprisonment. All were sure that before long, Satanta would sing the Kiowa death chant and somehow kill himself . . .

Buffalo Killer had paused to refill his pipe. Sundance waited patiently.

They had been lucky in the hunt, Buffalo Killer continued. They'd found a hidden grove with a spring in it where a small herd of buffalo grazed, and had made good kills. Also, the antelope had been more plentiful than usual. They soon had all the meat their horses could pack home, so they'd started back with it and the pony herd.

They wanted to return to their village as soon as possible so the meat wouldn't spoil. But Buffalo Killer had paused near Fort Sill and sent one of his braves, who was jestingly called Loves Many Squaws, for obvious reasons. Loves Many Squaws had attended a mission school for a time and spoke some English. He was to swap pelts for tobacco, calico and beads for the women at the trading post near the Fort. But chiefly he was to see if he could find out if Roland, the white boy, had come in. This had to be done most carefully so as not to cause the Osages any trouble. There would be Indians hanging around the post who would know.

As far as Loves Many Squaws could discover, no white boy had been reported as having ridden in from the Strip. Those who hung around the Fort would certainly know.

Buffalo Killer had been disturbed at this; it sounded as if Roland had spoken with a white man's usual forked tongue when he'd said he'd give himself up. While he was in the store, Loves Many Squaws had seen a man, a white man, come in and nail up circulars, offering rewards for the capture, dead or alive, of Sundance.

"I'd like to talk with Loves Many Squaws," said

Sundance.

"He's out now guarding the pack horses and pony herd, but I'll call him in."

Loves Many Squaws was a tall, lithe young brave with an easy way about him; Sundance could see why women would like him.

Sundance had seen him when he'd come in to eat, then gone back to his duties as a herd guard. An Indian, as he knew, seldom volunteered information unless asked, and Loves Many Squaws had not told him anything about being at the trading post and seeing the Wanted bills posted.

Now the young brave squatted, and Buffalo Killer handed him a pipe.

"When you were at the store, you say you saw a white man come in and hang up posters offering large rewards for my capture," began Sundance.

Loves Many Squaws puffed on the pipe, and then nodded.

"What did this *wasichu* look like?"

"He looked like a grizzly bear," replied Loves Many Squaws.

Buffalo Killer smiled. "Loves Many Squaws is a fine liar, as only too many pretty squaws have found out. He told me this, too, but how could a man look like a grizzly bear?"

"I have met one," said Sundance.

So Franz Berger was ahead of him. He would have to be doubly wary. Berger must have ridden through the main wagon road between Fort Smith and Fort Sill. He had probably guessed which way Sundance would head and hoped to trap him. Sundance had been traveling slowly, avoiding open areas, and had taken his time.

SEVEN

He decided to spend the night with his Osage friends and think over what his next move should be. Roland had eeled away again and there was no telling where he would end up next. Berger would be hunting the boy as well as looking for Sundance. One thing was certain, Roland had no intention of going back to his stepfather if he could help it. Too, he was probably having a really good time. No studies, no discipline, just sport among the Indians, with whom he had a genius for establishing instant rapport.

Comfortably fed, Sundance spread his blankets with the Osages. He unsaddled Eagle so the appaloosa could graze and drink as he pleased.

He slept soundly. At dawn, Buffalo Hunter ordered coffee made; Loves Many Squaws had brought some from the trading post. They had antelope steaks and soda biscuits, and the Osages prepared to hurry on to their village.

Sundance cautioned Buffalo Killer not to tell any

white men they'd seen him, although he knew it wasn't necessary, since no Indian would betray his friend.

He thanked Buffalo Killer and the rest for their hospitality. Saddling Eagle, he arranged his parfleche bags and bedroll, and began checking his weapons. The Osage exclaimed over his beautiful bow and the specially made arrows, the ivory-handled Colt and the repeating Henry rifle. Weapons were of prime importance to them, for hunting, defense and war.

The big question was, which way exactly would Roland head next? It was unlikely he'd turn around and go home; from all reports, Roland was having a grand time of it, and so far, all the savages he had encountered had treated him like a prince, spoiled him and made much of him. Roland was now clad as an Indian and riding an Indian pony. He would be tanned dark enough so that at a distance he'd look like an Indian lad.

Roland had failed to go to Fort Sill, as Buffalo Killer had discovered on his return from the Texas Panhandle. The Fort lay somewhat southwest of Sundance's present position; when he'd met the Osages, they were almost back home.

Like Roland, Sundance would shun Fort Sill. There would be the blood-money hunters looking for him, and almost any white man with a gun might try to arrest him. Though he was in Indian getup, the big appaloosa, well-known to Franz Berger, would be recognized a long way off, and Berger had evidently assumed personal command of the search for Sundance. Berger had come close to killing him twice, first on the Choctaw Plains, then at Froleiks' home in Fort Smith.

And Sundance did not underestimate Berger. He was clever and he was a tough, wily opponent with ample funds to pay for and command as many gunhands as he required.

Many young whites, not much older than Roland, had run off from homes in the East and Midwest, intrigued by the reported romance and excitement of cowboy and Indian fighter life. The magic goal was Texas and most of them would head· for the Lone Star State. Roland would be no exception; he'd showed this by running westward. A bright boy, he'd picked up lore and knowledge from his Indian friends and how to fend for himself in the wilds, and he was extremely bold and daring for his age.

Sundance knew all this territory from his youth and from later experience. His own tribe, the Southern Cheyenne, had ranged through here and through the Texas Panhandle, hunting bison and other game. The Cheyenne had been friendly with the Comanches and the Kiowas, which had long dominated the great plains of the Southwest.

Roland had a pony, and would stay near water. The sun was his compass. He'd passed north of Fort Sill, and that meant he would soon strike one of the numerous streams flowing into the North Fork of the Red River. And if he pushed south a few miles, he would come to some creek which would lead him to the Prairie Dog Town Fork of the Red. The boy could catch fish in the shallows, maybe trap small game. The Indians had taught him there were many berries and roots to eat.

Sundance could no longer always ride in cover, for he was coming to the open pasturelands. He'd have to depend on contours and keep a sharp eye out for possible enemies.

The day warmed and he pushed on, eyes flicking from one flank to the other. He sighted many bunches of cattle and some mustang bands, and in the distance, a couple of smokes which showed where homes stood. He was feeling his way, and would hope to meet some Indians who might have seen Roland.

At sundown, he camped by a small stream for the night. Buffalo Killer had given him some strips of buffalo meat, and he built a fire of dry sticks, the little smoke they gave off broken by the leaves on the limbs of a big cottonwood. He enjoyed a good meal, and made ready to sleep. He could always bring down game with his bow and arrows, so no gun explosions would attract anybody to his position.

In the fresh dawn, he saddled Eagle and prepared to move on toward the Panhandle. Fort Sill was now behind him, but there was always a chance of running into a cavalry patrol. The Army, too, would have been alerted to be on the watch for the tall Indian with flaxen hair on a big appaloosa stallion.

The sun grew hot as he rode on; he sighted a meandering line of growth marking the course of a creek.

He headed for this across rolling land where the coarse, nourishing grama grass dominated, excellent fodder for the buffalo, for cows and horses. He could at least use the growth along the stream as partial cover. Eagle needed a drink, and so did he.

Alamos, hackaberry bushes, pecans, flowering bush, and patches of tall bluestem grew near the creek. There was a small brush dam which formed a natural pool, and Eagle waded in as Sundance got down. When the appaloosa had drunk his fill, he began to crop at the bluestem, a grass much favored by grazing animals. Sundance saw wild ducks up the stream; he also noted swamp blackbirds, kingfishers busy hunting food, and wild canaries flitting in the thick brush. Water drew life, all forms of life; the predators came not only to drink but to catch prey, which also had to drink. There would be muskrats, otter, and in this country there were the clever coyotes ever looking for a meal; rabbits, leavings from a cougar's feast, they were always hungry.

And there were the insects, flies, mosquitoes, ticks, fulfilling their roles in the delicate balance of mighty Nature. In the pools were fish and frogs, turtles, and Sundance was happy, in these surroundings. He had been raised and had lived in the wilds; it was home to him.

He dried himself, put on his loincloth and moccasins, bound his hair with the snakeskin band. He stretched out, resting, letting Eagle graze, and figuring out his next move. This spot was an Indian camping ground, where they would pause to water their mustangs, drink, rest for a time before hurrying on toward the great war trail which slanted across the Panhandle and the Staked Plain, across the Pecos and south into old Mexico. For hundreds of years the Comanches and Kiowas had raided this way, running off horses, kidnaping young Mexican women for brides and for their own pleasure.

West rose the steep escarpment of the Llano Estacado, the Staked Plain.

He sighted a large jackrabbit, and reaching for his bow, nocked an arrow into the string. Waiting, still as a statue, he let the rabbit come close enough, then killed it with his arrow. He retrieved the arrow, bled the still-warm body, and secured it to his saddle. It would make a meal when he stopped for the night.

As he'd ridden, he'd kept hunting for some sign of Roland. The pony tracks would be smaller than those of the usual mustang, but the pony had been unshod, and with the light weight of a boy on its back, would leave few impressions in dry ground.

The land seemed limitless. And though it looked flat, it wasn't. It was a static ocean, long rises and troughs between, like a mighty sea.

Near the pool, the earth was softer but while there were plenty of tracks, both of cattle and horses, as well as of wild critters, he couldn't pick out any that might have been left by Roland's pony. Maybe he'd guessed wrong.

But he'd go on, and perhaps eventually come upon the boy's trail.

The sun was lowering in the vast arc of the sky as he rode along. It was in his eyes, and he lowered his head to keep the glare from blinding him.

He held Eagle to an easy but moving pace. If he found no sign of Roland, he decided next morning to cross over to the next creek valley. The boy might have followed that.

He skinned and cooked the rabbit for supper before sleeping. He bathed again in the stream, saddled Eagle, fixed his packs in the morning and left the creek valley, crossing northwest toward another branch of the Prairie Dog Fork of the Red.

He passed old buffalo wallows, where the mighty beasts had rolled in the dust to rid their hides of vermin. Now and then he saw the whitened skulls and bones of the bison, left by the murderous white hunters who had, in a decade, just about destroyed the chief source of food, shelter and clothing for the Plains Indians, for the Sioux and for the Cheyennes . . .

The slope was somewhat steep as he rode out of the valley, and looked down into the next depression. He glanced all around, carefully; he didn't like being outlined thus against the blue sky.

He pushed Eagle down the long decline toward the stream, which was a mile away. In between he saw some coarse mullein weed, prevalent in the region; as he approached, he noted the red clay bank of a deep arroyo. When there was a cloudburst, the arroyo might turn into a raging torrent, and this was tornado country as well.

As he surveyed the landscape, he was suddenly startled as something flashed in the sun, a brilliant, blinding flash that lasted but an instant.

But he knew what it was. Someone was lying up there behind an outcrop of red rock, watching him with binoculars. He at once lowered his head and picked up speed, hoping to reach the cover of the creek growth.

A heavy rifle bullet shrieked over his head; another plugged into the dirt, kicking up gravel. As he veered, he was fired on by a second hidden marksman, and he started to swing around, intending to gallop back to the stream he'd left.

He saw three cowboys ·flogging their horses after him. There were others coming at him now, riding, whooping it up, and opening fire at long distance with carbines. Cut off from retreat, he swung again and pelted toward the cover of the creek toward which he'd been heading.

Several riders broke out of the growth and galloped toward him.

Sundance knew he was surrounded. They had encircled him on the open plain and now there was no retreat.

Only one thing to do, and he instantly reined the appaloosa toward the arroyo. He found the shallow end, and jumping down, led Eagle as fast as he dared down the rocky slope to the bottom. There had been a pond there but it had dried up; only dried, dead weeds and a few bunches of grama grew about the cracked surface showing where the water had been.

For the moment, they couldn't kill Eagle or Sundance. He pulled the repeating Henry from its boot, threw the belt of ammunition for it over a shoulder; he had the short bow and quiver over the other. With these weapons, and with his big Colt, he could hold them off for a time. After dark, he might be able to break free, although then they would be able to creep up, close on his position.

He padded back to a point where he could just see over the top of the arroyo. They were still coming, and he threw the Henry to his shoulder and opened fire. He made a hit; a mustang fell, the rider jumping free, losing his carbine as he landed.

At a quick glance, these fellows looked like cowmen, not gunhands or outlaws.

A few shots from the Henry, and they lost their first enthusiasm about coming up with Sundance. He counted a dozen riding a half circle toward him, well spread. They didn't like the leaden hornets he sent at them, and they swung, zigzagging back out of easy range. Some of them wasted bullets which only sang over the dry split in the land, or skidded over in the red dirt.

He moved to the opposite side and found a spot where he could check that way. More of them, and they were closing in; he fired at them, and like the others, they turned and waited, out of range.

However, Sundance was boxed in, trapped.

It was very hot below the surface of the ground, for there was no movement of air. Sundance had to keep watch, first on one side, then on the other. The cowboys had dismounted, and were smoking, and he decided they were waiting for something.

He tried to figure it out. These were not blood-money hunters; they acted more like a posse, or a band of cowmen after stock thieves. Why should they bother with a lone Indian?

He had only his own horse, but then, the appaloosa was a distinctive animal and would easily be recognized even at a distance, particularly with binoculars. Someone had sighted him with field glasses, and given the signal to encircle him.

Only the deep arroyo had saved him from being shot down. He might have killed some of them, but they could have hit Eagle and then picked off Sundance.

He could only wait. Perhaps after dark—but there was a half moon which would come up, and they could close in, too, in the night.

Two uncomfortable hours passed by. An occasional long distance shot told Sundance they were still watching. He endured the discomfort with an Indian's stoic patience.

And suddenly he was startled. A deep voice spoke to him, amplified by a megaphone.

"Sundance! Hear me. Surrender yourself. You cannot get avay—" There it was, "avay."

Franz Berger had caught up with him again.

EIGHT

Grudgingly, Sundance had to admire Berger's strategy. Once again, as Berger had done when Sundance was headed for Fort Smith, Adolf Froleiks' partner and field general had outguessed him. Somehow, Berger's clever mind had figured which direction Sundance would take and had managed to drive in and cut him off.

The cowmen were still something of a mystery; of course, Berger might have collected them, offering to pay and to give them the reward for Sundance's capture. It was unusual for such a large band of men to gather together; it had proved very handy for Berger. He didn't doubt that his enemy had a few gunhands along too, and as soon as news spread that Sundance was cornered, the blood-money hunters would be drawn to the spot like flies to a decaying carcass . . .

Berger was bellowing at him again through his megaphone:

"Come out vith your hands raised, Sundance," he

ordered. "Ve haff you surrounded!"

Sundance set his jaw and inched to the brink of the arroyo, the loaded repeating Henry gripped in his big hands.

If he could kill Franz Berger, that would be some satisfaction, even though the cowmen might get him later.

Well back out of easy range he saw a large gray stallion, saddle on its back. And the sun glinted on the metal rim of the megaphone horn. Berger was standing behind his horse, and there were three or four other animals, their riders back of them, so that if Sundance opened up on Berger, the others would be hit first.

He'd considered shooting down the gray and then hoping to nail Berger when his horse fell.

But Franz Berger was too crafty for that.

Sundance held his fire. He'd only waste ammunition.

They were taking it easy out there, smoking, squatting with their reins loosely held. Somebody was passing a flask around.

He heard Eagle coming slowly toward him, and dropped to speak to his horse. The appaloosa was wet and there was foam on his lips. He wanted water; the heat had begun to tell on the animal.

Sundance patted the damp neck and Eagle nuzzled his hand. The man pointed and after a moment's hesitation, the horse lowered his head and plodded back to the bottom of the arroyo. The clay sides were baked and acted like the reflecting sides of an oven.

Well, he'd have to make a stab at escape after dark fell. But he knew that Franz Berger would figure on that, draw his men in, keep them on their bellies; they would cover both ends of the arroyo, and he would have to show against the sky as he emerged.

Better to die fighting though, than to be trapped like a wild animal. Berger would probably think up means of forcing him out, if he didn't come, maybe with smoke or powder.

Grimly, Sundance waited, leaning against the warm clay and thinking of past triumphs, of his loves, and particularly of Barbara Colfax. She was in Washington, working for the Indian interests, financed chiefly by Sundance's contributions, which also paid for the attorney fighting the Indian Ring who had grown fat with profits from thieving contracts and millions of dollars of Federal monies supposed to be given to the Indians.

He wondered if his allies had yet discovered what Adolf Froleiks was up to as he pulled political strings and offered bribes to influential Senators and members of the House.

He'd never find out, now, that seemed obvious.

He set his jaw, and the hatchet face seemed frozen in stone. He would never show fear, but he would die as a Cheyenne warrior should.

His mouth felt like dry flannel, and he slipped back; Eagle stood dejectedly, head down. Sundance found his canteen, which he'd filled at the creek to the south. He took a swallow, and then drew a bandana from his saddlebag. He wet this, trying not to spill a drop, and squeezed a dribble into Eagle's mouth, the stallion eagerly sucking in the moisture. Sundance repeated this process several times; no use saving any for himself. He intended to make a break for it when dark fell.

The arroyo ran roughly from west to east, as did most of the streams in the region. The eastern end was somewhat steeper than the western entrance to the split in the earth; he could lead Eagle up it, but at the western end he could mount and ride up the slide to the surface of the rolling plain. North was the next creek, perhaps half a mile away. If he could reach the thick growth along the water-course—

He was well aware he had little chance of making it. His respect for Franz Berger's cunning had increased and by now, he was sure that Berger would have figured out exactly what Jim Sundance would attempt. It was the only move the desperate, trapped Sundance could make. So, Berger would have the narrow gaps out of the arroyo tightly plugged, and a volley of death would cut the man and the magnificent appaloosa to shreds as they emerged from the deep cut.

Below the surface of the ground, Sundance could see the pale shape of the lopsided moon; when the sun set, it would offer enough light for the enemy to see his dark figure as he rode out of the arroyo.

The fine Henry repeating rifle in one big hand, he started back to a point where he could take an occasional peek at his foes, waiting until the moment came to make their kill. If only he could take Franz Berger with him! That would be something. But knowing the man who looked like a grizzly bear, as Loves Many Squaws had said, Sundance was sure that Berger would be quite safe when the quarry rode from the trap. Berger would be to the rear, directing operations like a field general, and without a doubt shielded not only by other men but by a bulwark of held horses.

He carefully peeked between two rocks sticking from the clay on the south brink of the arroyo. The waiting men, well back out of range, had secured their mounts, but left them saddled and ready to ride. They had started a fire which gave off a column of grayish smoke, and had evidently brought along meat and were boiling water for coffee, water brought from the creek bank behind them.

Some were passing flasks around, others smoking quirlies, chatting together, taking it easy.

The moments dragged; they seemed interminable to the besieged man. He wondered if it might not be better to make his dash for the north creek now, while they were lying back. He might have a better chance, though they had high-powered rifles and a couple were watching the arroyo. They had positioned the rifles on forked sticks driven into the ground, like buffalo hunters setting up a kill. In fact, Sundance saw that one was a long-barreled Sharps 50-caliber, a buffalo gun. It could kill a buffalo bull at long range, and they would aim at the big appaloosa and set Sundance afoot. Then they could pick him off as he dashed for the creek cover.

Anyway—

He saw one of the men in the main bunch stand up and wave, toward the meandering line of growth along the stream. As he watched, he caught the glint of the sunlight on a rifle barrel. Berger had thought of that, as he anticipated everything, every move Sundance might make. He had two or three sharpshooters hidden there, just in case the trapped man attempted to ride for it before dark. Berger had sent them well around, and Sundance hadn't seen them making the wide circle, for his vision was too restricted.

Well, he should have known Berger better than to think the man would leave any possible loophole in his trap.

Slowly, the sun dropped lower. Far in the distance was the escarpment of the Staked Plain, but this was cut off by the static wave between Sundance's position and the cliffs of the Llano Estacado.

He went back to check again on his weapons and on his equipment. He decided he would die as a Cheyenne warrior. He opened one of the parfleche bags and carefully drew forth his ceremonial headdress and delicately shook it out. The Cheyenne war bonnet was resplendent with beadwork and eagle feathers, the beaded headband decorated with conchas and ermine tails. When he was only twenty years of age, Sundance had earned the right to wear such a bonnet.

He had his short, curved bow of juniper wood lashed with sinew and tipped with buffalo horn, and ran his fingers down the loose bowstring to make sure it had no defect. This was the first weapon Sundance had learned to use and it had tremendous power. He could send an arrow for four hundred yards, and at closer distances, more than once had driven a shaft through a running bison—or a man. The string was plaited sinew from the shoulder tendon of a bull buffalo. He tightened the bowstring, setting the loose end in its niche, ready for instant use. He would carry it and his panther-skin quiver over one shoulder. He had the fully loaded repeating Henry; the Colt sixgun and the Bowie were ready in his belt. He also stuck his ax in his belt, and now he was fully armed.

He found some black dye and painted his face and torso with the proper streaks. This was war paint, and it meant death, death to any enemy who dared oppose him.

Taking off the rattlesnake headband, he carefully set the beautiful war bonnet on his hair; though he'd cropped some of his hair in Fort Smith, it was growing fast, and would soon flow over his broad shoulders . . .

Sundance laid his shield by him as he squatted down. The shield was not quite three feet in diameter, a circle of steam-warped juniper covered with dried, shrunken hide from the neck of a big buffalo bull. The hide was almost hard as iron. Next came a thick layer of dried grama grass, then a layer of deerskin, with a Thunderbird emblem painted on it. Such a shield would turn an arrow and even a light bullet, although a heavy rifle or a .50-caliber slug from a Sharps buffalo gun would penetrate it. Yet the shield, to a Cheyenne Dog Soldier, was sacred and powerful medicine. The Thunderbird shield was his warrior's luck, a spiritual as well as physical protection in combat, such as a white man's Bible or a St. Christopher medal.

When he raised it, six long tufts of hair dangled from it: scalps. Three were coarse and black, the scalps of Indians, while the other three were softer, finer, a bit shorter, one brown, one reddish, the third as yellow as his own hair. These were the scalps of the six men who had murdered his father, Nicholas Sundance, and his mother, Smiling Woman, on the trail out of Bent's Fort.

Sundance had stayed behind at the fort to watch

the horse races, and next day, the young son had ridden hard to overtake his parents, only to find their bodies, shot and scalped, some thirty miles north of the Arkansas. The killers had violated his mother before slaying her.

He'd read the sign, three Pawnees, three white derelicts who were prairie tramps. They'd left Bent's Fort shortly after the departure of Jim's parents. The buzzards had already been at the bodies of his loved ones. Sundance had wrapped the remains in buffalo hides and secured them in the branches of trees, according to Indian custom. Then he'd set out, and he had hunted down the six murderers. They had all died slowly, painfully, once Sundance had found them . . .

That was the past. He didn't believe he had much of a future left now, with Berger waiting to pounce on him. He looked upward; he knew the Great Spirit had taken his parents to Him. And Sundance prayed he would be found worthy to join them.

He stood erect, and gave Eagle the last drops of water from his canteen. He laced his parfleche bags, made certain they were secure with his pack. He felt no pangs of hunger as he made ready for his final charge.

He checked the cinches on the mighty appaloosa. Eagle would probably die with him, for they would send a terrific fusillade at him, blindly as they saw him emerge from the end of the arroyo. Some of the metal would hit the horse, and if Eagle wasn't killed instantly, they would have to shoot him since he'd have little chance of recovery.

Weapons ready, Sundance led the drooping appaloosa toward the shallower end of the cut. He could see the sun, enlarging, turning reddish as it prepared to set. The glint was blinding to his eyes and he looked away to protect his vision from blurring.

He peeked between the two rocks. Franz Berger's allies had finished eating, drinking and smoking. He watched as some made sure rifles and revolvers were loaded. Cinches were being pulled up tight and the crew had spread out, making ready for the charge.

The moment the sun disappeared, they would start. He could see them looking over toward the arroyo. And he picked out the burly, bearded Berger, moving from man to man, giving final instructions.

But even at such a distance, Berger took no chance a lucky slug from the arroyo would find him. Most of the time he kept his horse as a shield, and Sundance had only tantalizing glimpses of his powerful enemy.

The cookfire had about died off; only a faint spiral of smoke rose. It rose straight upward, for the warm breeze had entirely died out. The world seemed preternaturally quiet to the besieged Sundance, crouched in the arroyo.

The sun was a huge crimson orb; it seemed to rest on the summit of the rise to the west.

And Jim Sundance prepared to die.

NINE

Sundance wondered if Hell was any hotter than the spot he was in. An ordinary man would have been overcome by the oven-like heat.

He thought of the snowy reaches of the Rockies and the Sierras, and how the Cheyennes had wintered, their tepees set firmly in the deep snows. Winter hadn't been too bad for the Indians, not if they had dried and stored enough meat and berries and roots. Fires would be kept burning in the wigwam centers, and the younger braves would sometimes venture out through the snow to hunt for deer or antelope in protective ravines where the north wind blew most of the snow from the grasses and they could find fodder and stay alive until Spring.

It had all been good, a good life . . .

Suddenly, a rifle shot split the still air, echoing through the shallow valley.

Sundance was surprised; he glanced through the peephole between the rocks. There was unusual activity among the white men, who had thrown reins over their shoulders, and were raising their rifles.

He was puzzled; it was too soon for them to charge the arroyo, and anyhow, they were all looking westward, shading their eyes against the blinding sun by pulling down their Stetson brims. He heard shouting, and above the yells of the rest, the bull roar of Franz Berger's voice bellowing commands.

Sundance ran to the lower end of the arroyo; he crouched, putting his hand over his eyes and not looking directly at the crimson sun.

Now he caught the drum of many hooves, and next, fierce war whoops. Out of that brilliant, blinding sunlight a line of wild riders broke, heading straight for the white camp, screaming bloodthirsty cries.

They zigzagged as they came, reckless in their insane speed. Sundance saw them, twenty to thirty anyhow, bareback on shaggy mustangs, kicking heels against the ponies' ribs as they urged their horses on.

They were naked to the waist, torsos gleaming with grease rubbed on—in hand-to-hand combat, it was practically impossible to get a grip on an arm. Their legs were cased in deerskin, heel tassels sweeping the ground, and they rode high on the withers, using only a piece of rope as a guiding rein. Most of them had rawhide loops around the mustangs' necks so they could hang on, shoot an arrow or rifle under the animal as they sped along.

And now they were close enough so Sundance could make out some of the fierce faces. The streaks on the faces were black, as was Sundance's, war paint, the color of Death. Their bodies, too, had designs painted on them, and Sundance, who knew all the tribes, recognized the tribal marks.

Kiowas!

The most deadly Plains warriors known, even surpassing the Comanches. The Cheyennes, Comanches, Arapahoes and Apaches were all more numerous, but there was an inborn deadliness about the Kiowas which made them more dangerous, man for man, than any other Plains tribe.

The Kiowas had killed more white men, in proportion to their numbers, than any western tribe. And the arrest and imprisonment of their greatest living chief, Satanta, had aroused them like giant hornets, hornets whose sting spelled death.

They had caught the white men with Berger off guard, out in the open. The nearest cover was back to the south, in the trees and heavy brush of the creek; they could dismount, lie just below the bank, and defend themselves.

Some of them thought of it right away, and leaping to saddle, retreated from the rapidly growing battle.

Others threw themselves flat, hastily opening fire on the charging Kiowas. The savages zigzagged, riding like insane centaurs. They swept in closer and closer, attempting to circle the white foe. A brave would grasp the rawhide circlet, keep a moccasined foot over his mustang's back, and fire under the animal's belly.

An Indian's horse was hit by cooler heads among the cowmen. The brave landed running and without a pause, leaped up behind a comrade who was passing and gave him a hand up.

They never left their wounded or dead, not if it could be helped. It would be a badge of shame forever pinned on a man if he deserted a comrade or left the body lying on the field.

The din was terrific. Hooves pounded, raising clouds of reddish dust. The Indians uttered blood-curdling whoops, and the guns of both sides blasted the hot air of the late afternoon. Many of the savages had carbines, others were using the bow and arrow.

A feathered shaft drove deep into the belly of a big chestnut, and the horse screamed and fell, kicking in agony; Sundance thought there was nothing worse than hearing the cries of a badly hurt horse. A Kiowa was shot through the body; he flew off his pony as the critter veered, nostrils flaring. The Indian landed on his head, breaking his neck. A companion swept up his body, leaning far to one side as he swept by, and carried the dead man out of the battle.

The pounding lines of the Kiowas drew ever closer to the enemy, and several of the white men's mounts were hit.

A warwhoop blasting from his dry throat, heart racing and blood pounding with the excitement of the battle, Sundance leaped on the appaloosa and rode up the slide onto the plain. He charged straight at the huddled group of defenders.

Then he saw a powerful chestnut stallion, a hulking figure low over the saddle, galloping for cover along the creek to the south.

It was Franz Berger. Sundance aimed the Henry at the fleeing enemy and fired twice, but the distance was long, and the jolting of the stallion under him spoiled his aim. He could see his slugs kick up dirt to one side or the other of Berger, and now bullets from the white-eyes still in the open began shrieking about him. He swerved, Indian-fashion, and the Kiowas whooped to him. He raised his rifle overhead, in a sign of friendship and brotherhood. They knew he was a Cheyenne; he figured the Kiowas could have seen him in the arroyo from the crest behind which they had been lurking, awaiting the signal from their chief to charge out of the blinding sunlight.

The Kiowas were drawing closer, and the survivors of the party still out on the plain jumped on unwounded horses and fled for safety toward the south creek, followed by bullets, arrows and triumphant shouts from the warriors.

Sundance, blood heated with hate for Franz Berger, the long siege in the baking oven of that arroyo and the excitement of battle, flew on, reckless of the chances. Only one other Indian, some yards off to his left, dared keep charging. Sundance knew at a glance he was a chief; he was large for a Kiowa, naked torso and face streaked with paint which told Sundance his standing as a great warrior. The chief rode a long-limbed pinto, a beautiful animal; the pinto was shod, larger than the usual Indian mustang, and undoubtedly stolen from a white ranch.

The chief made the sign of friendship and Sundance replied.

They were charging into the face of death, for now the white men had left their saddles and bellied along the screened bank of the stream. They would have a steady rest from which to aim and shoot, and a moment later, the paint horse was hit and went crashing hard to the red earth, landing hard on his side and kicking in deadly agony.

The Kiowa had jumped off as his mount fell under him. He was jolted, and crouched for a moment; the men over at the creek concentrated fire on him, and he might have died, but Sundance swerved, leaned way over to one side, and held out a strong arm. The Kiowa grasped it and Sundance pulled him up, the chief leaping up before him.

Sundance pivoted the appaloosa and zigzagged from the spot, followed by bullets from Berger's party.

A few shots rang out from the north creek; most of the Indians had turned that way. They'd smashed the cowmen, hurt them badly. Sundance saw three whites riding hell-for-leather along the north stream; they must be the sharpshooters Berger had posted over there to make sure of finishing him if somehow he had survived the ride out of the arroyo.

Eagle kept galloping toward the creek. Foam flecked the great horse's writhing lips. Sundance attempted to check the stallion's rush, but Eagle knew there was water over there and he was half-mad with thirst. He galloped on until he broke through the brush along the river and didn't stop till he was knee-deep in the stream. He put down his head and sucked in the cool liquid.

A couple of Indians came along the far bank of the creek, loosely gathering the Indian pony herd. Mustangs were caught up and the dead brave was secured over the back of one; the Kiowas had two men wounded, one seriously, and a comrade mounted behind him to hold him up as they took off, heading northeast. The other man, who'd been hit in the fleshy part of the thigh, was able to stay aboard.

109

The young chief, the man Sundance had picked up, spoke to him in Kiowa. Sundance could speak some Kiowa, but it was an outlandish tongue. The jest was that even two Kiowas talking together had to use some sign language to make themselves understood by one another. The lordly, arrogant Comanches never bothered to learn Kiowa, so the Kiowas had to speak Comanche.

Sundance replied to the chief's thanks; he was a Cheyenne, he said, a *Hevataniu*. And Sundance told the chief he was of the *Is-sio-me-tan-iu* band.

"It is good," said the chief, lapsing into Comanche.

Eagle, having satisfied his first craving for water, responded to his rider's urging and splashed across the creek, which was belly-deep in its center. Sundance didn't want the stallion to drink too much while he was overheated, and pushed Eagle up on the north bank.

The firing had subsided. The cowmen, led and inspired by Franz Berger, had had enough fighting for the time being, and were seeing to their wounded.

A horse was cut out and brought over for the chief whom Sundance had picked up on the battlefield. The Kiowa transferred to the back of the chestnut, which had shaggy hair and a white foreleg. He signalled, and the main party of his braves started riding off after the first few who had charge of the injured and the dead.

A couple of braves waved bloody scalps overhead, then stuck them on their lances.

The chief and Sundance brought up the rear of the war party, talking as they rode. "We saw you in

110

the arroyo," said the Kiowa. "We had heard gunfire and it drew us to the spot earlier. You see, a large party of young braves was with me. We were raiding the ranches of the accursed white-eyes, and the ones you fought back there were trailing us, for we'd stolen many of their horses, captured three white women, and killed some men who fought us."

Sundance saw the picture. Franz Berger, trailing Sundance, had made a smart guess which way he'd go. He'd met the posse of cowmen and enlisted them, probably lied, telling them Sundance was a chief who'd led the raids on their homes.

Berger had come close to winning—this time. Sundance set his jaw. Well, it would be different, when he next came near to the man who looked like a grizzly bear and who was one of the two prime enemies he'd met, the other being Adolf Froleiks.

He was still smarting from being outguessed by Berger, and the stay in the arroyo hadn't helped abate his hate.

He saw the party leaving the creek, and signalled that he must have water. He turned to the stream, got down, and let Eagle drink more, while he waded in and drank his fill, cooled his face with water and filled his empty canteen.

The young Kiowa chief waited for him till he was ready to ride again. His name, he said, was Tall Tree as it would be said in English translation. The Kiowa band to which he belonged was hidden deep in the Territory—as Sundance knew, Indian tribes would only gather for ceremonies and tribal rites. Otherwise, they would split up into smaller groups, for hunting and for sanitary reasons. It was so with all the tribes. Sometimes there would be thirty or forty different wandering bands, often far apart. They would meet on occasion, or two or three bands would supply warriors who wished to go on a raid. An Indian would follow only a chief whom he respected and there was no discipline as there was in white armies. Unless a chief's orders were obeyed, he was no longer considered a leader.

"You know," continued Tall Tree, as they rode on after the band in the failing daylight, "I had twice as many braves with me when we set out. But the *wasichun* were too close to us, and so I sent some of my men ahead with the stolen horses and the captives. Then I led this party off to trick the white men and hide the real trail."

A typical Indian ruse, thought Sundance, nodding. It often proved surprisingly effective. Unless led by a most experienced tracker and a man used to savage tricks, the usual white posse would pick the wrong fork. The captives and stolen animals would be taken along a watercourse for some miles, while the decoys would leave an easier trail to follow.

"The Kiowas are furious," said Tall Tree. "First, Se-tan-gya, the white-eyes called him Satank, was trapped and soldiers killed him on the way to the white man's prison. Still, Se-tan-gya was very old, though when he was younger, he was the greatest chief of all the Kiowas. Then we turned to Se-tain-te (White Bear) but the whites called him Satanta. He was arrested, too, and spent two years in the prison, but then he was let go. But Se-tain-te was a bitter man and he lived only to kill the white-eyes. Now, the troopers have caught him again and it is said he will never, never return. The older chiefs say we must be cautious, but we younger men have sworn

112

to die fighting, and kill as many white-eyes as we can."

He glanced at the grim, hatchet face of the big man riding by him. Sundance swept off his war bonnet to wipe his sweaty brow.

Tall Tree nodded. "Yes, I was right. I told my braves you are the great Sundance!"

"I am Sundance. Satanta was a close friend of mine, and the greatest of chiefs. Satank, too, I knew well before he died."

"I am glad we came along in time. The whites meant to kill you."

"I came over this way looking for a white boy who ran away from home," explained Sundance.

"A white boy! Sundance, perhaps we caught him. He was riding an Indian pony along the north bank of this very creek, headed west, and we caught him several miles west of where we just had the fight. First we thought he was an Indian boy, for he was very brown and wore Osage garments. When we found he was white, some of my men wanted to kill him at once, but I said no, he showed no fear of us and he was a brave boy. So I sent him back with the party driving the stolen horses and the captive white girls. He will be hidden deep in the Territory, but you realize, if white soldiers approach, we must kill all white captives and hide their bodies. The soldiers would blame us all, slay our braves, squaws and children."

Sundance nodded. He knew how it was. Rather than be caught with white prisoners, the Kiowas would kill them and bury them deep in the wilds of the Nations.

Well, thought Sundance, he'd only been one creek

away as he'd trailed Roland.

And at last, he'd found Roland—almost, unless the lad managed to escape from the Kiowas. But that was unlikely; they would keep a close watch on him. But it would be touch and go, for Roland. If a troop of cavalry surprised the Kiowa camp, the savages would kill the boy to protect themselves.

TEN

While Sundance admired the fighting power of the Kiowas, they had another trait he didn't like. They were noted as the cruelest of torturers, and even the Quahada Comanches, proud as they were, admitted the Kiowas could outdo them along this line.

With his knowledge of history, Sundance was aware that when it came down to innate cruelty, the Spaniards and the Anglos would take the blue ribbons. But the Kiowas had devised means of keeping a suffering prisoner alive for many days, staked out, and praying only for the release that death would bring. One favorite way was to stick pine splinters into an arm, light them, and laugh as the person's flesh sizzled and burned; then they would do the same to the other arm, and later, one leg, then the other. The body would come next, and the torture dragged out, to the amusement of the squaws and warriors. Wrapping a naked man in the green hide of a skinned steer and letting it slowly shrink in the sun until the life was squeezed from the body was another, though this was also practiced by the Yaquis and other tribes.

Sundance was now willing to ride back into the Territory. Roland was somewhere in the hidden Kiowa camp, and he had yet to uncover what Froleiks and Berger were planning. And he had every intention of coming to grips with the man who looked like a grizzly, and with Froleiks, the man who had beaten Simone and her son, Roland. Fear of his stepfather was the prime motive for Roland running away.

Dark had fallen. The half-moon offerred enough light for the Kiowas to ride by, and they knew the trails. The Big Dipper, revolving as it did about the North Star, pointed the way for them, as it often did for cowboys on the cattle trails to Kansas.

Way in the distance they saw a few twinkling lights, a ranch. The Indian avoided all habitations; they were crossing broken pasture land now, and could pick up the pace, which had slowed in the forests. They would cross two of the Trails from Texas to the Arkansas and Kansas railheads, but the Trails were many miles wide, dictated as they were by grazing needs for the longhorns being slowly pushed northward . . .

Tall Tree had a deerskin pouch of pemmican. He offered it to Sundance, and as they rode as a rear guard, they ate, and Sundance and the Kiowa chief both had full canteens. They kept pushing northeastward all night, at an easy but distance-consuming pace.

When the first gray of the dawn showed in the sky ahead, they had reached good cover in forests, and had passed well to the north of Fort Sill.

Tall Tree ordered a brief halt to rest, drink and eat what they had left after their long raid into the Texas Panhandle. The wounded men suffered stoically, without any sign of what they felt. The dead brave had been secured over the back of a pony from the herd. Indians on long runs always had spare mounts with them. If a mustang was injured or killed, or spent, they could change over when they wished.

Now Tall Tree ordered three braves to cut spruce limbs and use them as drags. They must wipe out tracks, and all sign. As they reached a small river running in the direction they wished to travel, the Indians took to the shallows, for the water would hide their horse tracks.

Tall Tree was most careful about concealing their trail. He seemed to be an expert at this.

They finally left the stream, wiped out sign where they'd emerged, and Tall Tree moved the party through a dense pine woods. The dried brown needles carpeting the earth, inches deep, left little or no hint they'd passed through.

The Kiowas knew exactly where they were headed. The sun had come up and was on their left as they splashed across a small stream and weaved on through another patch of woods. In the distance, Sundance heard dogs barking. The Kiowa camp couldn't be far away.

Tall Tree, Sundance at his side, rode first into the encampment. Tepees stood along the north bank, and there were cooking holes dug outside, with stacks of dry wood ready. Three or four deer carcasses hung on limbs, out of the reach of the dogs.

Indian boys ran to greet the returning warriors,

beating off the barking curs with sticks. Tall Tree rode back and forth in the open space; by the sign, they knew that they had lost at least one man, and anxious squaws pressed forward, looking for their husbands and sweethearts.

As the pony with the corpse on it was slowly led into camp, a squaw began to keen, wailing in mourning for her loved one.

She drew her butcher knife from her belt and hacked off her black braids. Then she slashed her brown cheeks with the sharp blade, and blood flowed from the self-inflicted wounds. Her husband's body was carried off to a nearby grove and covered with a buffalo robe, and the squaw sat by it, keening and rocking back and forth in a paroxysm of grief.

This exhibit of emotion of the widow didn't surprise Sundance, for he had seen it often among other tribes, including his own, the Cheyennes. While the white men insisted that Indians were no better than wild beasts, they suffered as much for their lost loved ones as did any paleface, and certainly showed it more.

The squaws whose husbands had returned safely took their men's horses and led them off. They would see to their mates' comforts, and there would be first a dance to celebrate the victory of the returned war party, and then a feast.

A medicine man appeared. He was wearing a face mask and wore a wolf skin with legs and tail hanging from it. He carried two gourds with dried rattles from snakes on them, and he went into the lodges of the injured warriors to make magic incantations over them. Older squaws were preparing to mix poultices with which to bind the wounds.

The mustangs were herded off to be guarded by lads who had not gone on the raid with Tall Tree.

Older men squatted together in groups, smoking and talking together in low tones. They had not approved of the raids, for they knew the soldiers would hunt them down, searching for the white girls carried off, and they would punish not only the guilty but everybody in the village.

The Indians who had been on the raid went to their own lodges. Tall Tree introduced Sundance to his squaw, who was very pretty. Her name was Star Eyes and she welcomed her handsome husband with great joy, and her man's guest.

Tall Tree led Sundance to a secluded pool down the stream, Sundance calling to Eagle to follow. He removed his feathered headdress and carefully stowed it in its parfleche bag, lacing up the long pouch. Unsaddling the appaloosa, he let Eagle drink, and washed the big stallion down.

"Do you want the herd boys to guard him?" asked Tall Tree.

"No. He won't stray far and he'll come when I call."

Tall Tree marveled. "He is the greatest horse I have ever seen. And you, Sundance, you are the greatest warrior of all the Indian tribes. I wish you would stay and fight the white-eyes with us."

Sundance shook his head. "I am doing what I can to save something for our peoples," he said sadly. "After I've rested, I must leave."

Both men removed their moccasins and gear, and waded into the pool. They lay down, basking in the cool water for a time. Other braves who had been out on the long raid could be seen up and down the bank, as they washed the trail dust and battle stains from their lean brown bodies.

When they returned to Tall Tree's tepee, word had spread through the village that the famous Sundance had come to them, and that he had fought the whites in a hard battle in the Panhandle and had picked up Tall Tree, the chief of the party, when the chief's horse had been shot from under him. Young women would look at Sundance and then flush and lower their eyes, batting their lashes as an eligible squaw did when in the presence of a possible suitor she admired.

Tall Tree laughed. "You can take your pick of them, my friend," he said. "You impress them."

The young war chief lifted the flap of his tepee, inviting his honored guest to enter.

The two men sat down together, cross-legged in Indian fashion, on buffalo robes in the man's section of the tepee, where the husband kept his weapons and special belongings. Actually, the lodge belonged to the woman, as it did with the Sioux and Cheyennes. So did any offspring; they would be given their mother's surname. Occasionally a shrewish, scolding wife, married to a meek husband, would throw him out, his belongings after him. The other men would laugh at him but it was good-natured mirth . . .

Tall Tree filled a pipe, puffed at it, passed it to Sundance, who smoked and then handed it back to his host.

The morning was warm, and Star Eyes cooked at the outdoor fireplace. That night the feast and dance would take place. The warriors would dance about, describing and reenacting their feats in the battle and during the long raid.

Star Eyes brought the food to the two men in the lodge. There were strips of buffalo meat, flat cakes with dried berries in them, other delicacies. Tall Tree and Sundance ate with their fingers. A length of meat was put in the mouth and a bite size cut off with the man's knife. There was a drink made of fermented mare's milk and other ingredients; it had a pungent but not unpleasant taste.

Star Eyes did not eat with the men. She had gone outside to gossip with other squaws, and tell more about the famous guest her husband had brought to the lodge.

When they had finished eating, the men again smoked. Sundance and his friend were both sleepy from the long, hard ride and the meal. Both napped for a time, and when Sundance awoke, the afternoon was well along.

They went out again. The squaws were endlessly busy; they were now preparing for the great victory celebration that would take place after dark. Tall Tree and Sundance went again to bathe in the pool. Eagle came walking over to the bank; the appaloosa had grazed nearby, always within call. And up the line, the herd boys were watching the ponies.

Tall Tree dried himself, and pulled on his long deerskin leggings, and Sundance donned his moccasins and wrapped the rattlesnake band around his fair hair.

When they returned to the village, they saw groups of older men, sitting around and talking together.

So far, Sundance hadn't seen Roland. Tall Tree hadn't brought up the subject, after he'd informed

Sundance that Roland was in the village, and Sundance knew better than to press the matter until the proper time. Now, he asked.

"I haven't seen the white boy you said had been brought in with your other party, Tall Tree."

"Oh, he's with the herd boys. His mother has said the boys must keep an eye on him so he won't run away or be hurt. He is very fond of horses."

"His mother?"

"Oh yes, he has been adopted as a son by Wolftooth and his squaw Blue Flower. They had no children of their own. But now they have a fine son."

Sundance wasn't glad to hear this. A child adopted by Indians was looked upon and treated exactly as natural offspring. If he asked the couple to give up Roland, it would be the same as asking parents to surrender their only son. It was most unlikely they would be willing to trade or sell the boy.

"He's a brave boy, as I said," went on Tall Tree. "And he seems very happy with us."

Among the trees, on the far side of the creek, stood a lone tepee. There were three or four squaws watching; Sundance saw them go in and out, and he had no doubt that the three white women captured during the raid, and brought in by the first party which had also driven the stolen horses, were being held there. He knew that they would have been violated, many times, by now, probably on the trail to the village. Such a female belonged to the warrior who caught her, and he could keep her as a wife or trade her to another man if he wished. Wolftooth would have been with the Kiowas sent back to the village with the captives and stolen animals, while Tall Tree led his braves off to decoy the pursuing ranchers.

The brave who had been seriously wounded was still living, and the medicine men were busy with him; the second, whose wound had been superficial, was already up and about.

Large joints of meat were being roasted by the busy squaws, as they prepared for the feast. There would be other items, wild sweet potatoes, fermented drink, and flat breads.

Late in the afternoon, a group of boys rode out to spell the herd guards, and Sundance watched, squatted in front of Tall Tree's lodge. Soon four lads came in on their ponies. It was hard, at a distance, to pick out Roland. He was dressed as were his comrades, and he was so tanned by the sun that his skin looked like an Indian's. It was only when he came closer that Sundance could see he was a white boy. His features were pleasing, and he had large violet eyes with long lashes; they were his mother's eyes.

Sundance thought of Simone, the beautiful French woman waiting for him in Fort Smith. She had promised that she would give herself to him as a reward if he could bring back her beloved son to her.

Roland went to Wolftooth's lodge, which was past Tall Tree's tepee. Blue Flower, a small but pretty squaw, lovingly greeted her "son." She smiled at him and petted him and Roland kissed her, as a white child would a trusted parent.

Sundance had seen Wolftooth, a wiry, strong-jawed Kiowa brave. He was faced with a difficult problem. He didn't believe the couple would surrender or trade for Roland. The only course left was to steal the boy, but he'd have to see if Roland was

123

willing to go along with him. It would have to be done very carefully and stealthily, perhaps after the great victory feast that night, when the men and women would be sleeping off the celebration.

He would have to make preparations for this, and strolled through the camp; the people greeted him, watching the famed Sundance. On the pretext of checking his gear, he made everything ready, so he could saddle Eagle and be ready to run for it at the proper time.

Blue Flower fed Roland, making much of him. Sundance could see she already loved the boy dearly.

Finally the village crier came through the camp, banging on his skin drum. There was to be a great show, it was announced. Soon the audience gathered in a circle. Roland had disappeared into his parents' tepee.

Sundance joined the gathering, which laughed and joked as they waited for the show to begin. Indians had to devise their own entertainment; they had, often, a childlike sense of humor, sometimes cruel, but they could understand broad satire, and practical jokes.

Three very tough-looking braves came to the center of the stage. They had fiercely painted faces, black streaks on them, and down their bodies. All were armed to the teeth with lances, bows and arrows, carbines, and long butcher knives.

Suddenly Roland appeared. He, too, had war paint on his young face and there were humorous designs on his torso. He wore leggings with the seat cut out, so his bare bottom showed.

On the boy's head was a full warbonnet. But in

this case, they were not eagle feathers. Sundance recognized buzzard plumes, jay tail feathers, crow plumage. A couple of polecat tails hung down his naked back. The getup was enough to send the Kiowas into a paroxysm of laughter.

Roland carried a wooden ax or hatchet, a wooden scalping knife, and a wooden musket.

It was the first time Sundance had seen Roland's act. Evidently he'd elaborated on it, as he had found how he could amuse the savages everywhere he went. He seemed to be a born actor and was thoroughly enjoying himself.

The corners of Sundance's stern mouth turned up; he could see the burlesque of the performance, appreciate the crude humor.

Now Roland began his famous war dance. He put down his bonneted head and raised one foot after another, whirling as he began whooping it up. He would put a hand to his mouth, then take it away, as he uttered his ferocious cries, but as his voice hadn't yet dropped, it was a treble.

Suddenly he made his charge, jumping into the circle where the trio of warriors threatened him with lances.

He took on all three; the first one he stabbed at with the wooden lance was an acrobat; feigning to be slain, he did a complete back flip and lay doubled up. The second died, too, as Roland went for him. When he went down, he stuck up his rump and rested like a cow attempting to pull itself out of a bog.

The audience was now shrieking with laughter at the mock battle. Some rolled around, holding their bellies at the ridiculous performance. Roland whirled, finding the third scowling warrior almost upon him. He raised his wooden musket and shouted, "Bang!" The brave folded up, done for.

Roland began his victory dance; he'd copied it from what he'd seen in Indian camps, and perhaps in pictures he'd seen in books.

As he whirled about in the antic gyrations of triumph, suddenly he pulled out what looked like a scalp; it was really a piece of coyote skin. He raised it in triumph.

But the show wasn't over. Roland must have also enlisted some of his playmates, and half a dozen of them suddenly charged into the circle and came at him, whooping it up. Roland shot or stabbed them all, and then stood, one foot on the rump of the clown warrior.

The performance was over. The Kiowas were still laughing and applauding.

The audience broke up into small groups. The night would soon be upon them. As Sundance walked across the circle, Roland came close to him, on his way back to Blue Flower's tepee, not far from the creek.

Sundance spoke to him in English: "Roland. I am Sundance."

The boy looked up at the tall, hatchet-faced man with the scarred cheek and hair the color of new wheat. Sundance could see a strong resemblance to Simone in Roland's features.

"I know, you are Sundance, a famous warrior. You picked up Tall Tree in the fight."

"Your real mother is my friend, Roland. I've seen her in Fort Smith. Her heart is breaking because you've run away."

Roland looked miserable; he glanced at the

ground. "I—I love her, yes, I love my mother. But—I hate my stepfather. He beats me, but worse, he beats my mother when he's drunk. I—I hate Froleiks. I like the Indians; they are very good to me. But I would never fight them, I think they are wonderful people."

"You're a smart boy, Roland. You learn very quickly. But—don't you ever want to see your mother again?"

"Yes. I miss her more and more. I wish she could live with the Indians. She'd be much happier than she is with Froleiks. I can't bear to see her hurt. If I could I'd hit when he hits her."

Wolftooth had come up and stood behind them. He seemed puzzled at what was being said; he spoke no English. Blue Flower came and put her arm around Roland, hugging him to her bosom. "Come," she said in Comanche. "I will wash you clean and then I will feed you. You must go to sleep after that." She seemed very proud of her new son, who was already a celebrity as the camp's comic entertainer.

Sundance made the sign of peace to Wolftooth, who responded.

The tall man strolled on. He must snatch Roland, somehow, from the Kiowa camp. He hadn't had time to broach the subject of Roland running away with him, but when he had an opportunity, he'd have a really serious talk with Roland and point out his duty was to his natural mother. He'd detected a hint of homesickness in the boy, who loved Simone dearly and missed her.

He continued on toward the creek and made sure Eagle was close. The appaloosa caught his scent and came splashing through the water. Sundance stroked him, and spoke to the big stud.

He knew too much about the Kiowas to hope that Wolftooth and Blue Flower would sell him their new "son." The savages were primitive, and even Tall Tree, whose life he had saved during the fight with Franz Berger and the cowmen, would refuse to help take Roland from his Indian parents. Even to mention it would arouse suspicion in the camp.

Sundance squatted on his haunches, trying to figure it out. It would be very difficult to spirit Roland out of the village. The youth couldn't maintain enough speed for a long enough distance to outride the Kiowa braves.

True, Blue Flower and Wolftooth had set their lodge not far from the creek. But both would be sleeping in the tepee, and probably Blue Flower would have Roland snuggled close to her for warmth and comfort. The couple might even have Roland between them.

He'd need Roland's full cooperation to snake him out of the hostiles' village. He must have a start of several hours; then he might ride in the shallows to hide sign, but the Kiowas knew that ruse only too well and how to counter it.

Once he could get well away, Sundance intended to head for Osage range, and then hurry on to Tahlequah. There he could leave Roland in the care of Our Wise One. He'd cross the Arkansas and visit Tall Littleman.

By that time, the Cherokee wrangler should have an answer from Barbara Colfax in Washington and he would learn exactly what Adolf Froleiks, and his partner, Franz Berger, were planning as to Indian

Territory.

It was a most ticklish business, all in all. Berger was the major witness against Jim Sundance, accusing him of the murders. He would undoubtedly perjure himself in court and not confess that Sundance had only been defending himself on the Choctaw Plains, and in the yard that night at Froleiks's home in Fort Smith. And it was Berger who had posted the "Wanted" bulletins . . .

Sundance strolled back to the center of the village. Huge bonfires were being readied, and the meat was sizzling on the spits, odors appetizing in the cooling forest air. The squaws were very busy, preparing foods for the banquet. They would participate in the dances, and the braves who had been on the raids would reenact how they had vanquished the enemies killed and scalped.

He knew there was nothing he could do about the captive white women, not now. It was a sad thing, but the whites treated Indian girls even worse, raping them at will, deserting them.

Cruelty, thought Sundance, seemed part of Mankind's makeup.

Up the way, he saw several Indian boys teasing a young coyote they'd trapped. The unfortunate animal's jaws were tightly tied with rawhide thongs, and so were his paws, so he was helpless. Sundance realized what was going to happen later. The coyote would be skinned alive and then turned loose; the frenzied critter's antics before it died would bring gales of laughter from the assemblage. It was a favorite amusement of the Kiowas. As he stood watching, Roland, who had removed his bonnet and getup, came up beside him.

Roland didn't laugh; he said, "I don't like that. I love animals; it's all right to kill them for food, but not to torture them. One of the Cherokee boys had a pet coyote and we could pat it like a dog."

Roland spoke in English, and Sundance answered in the same language. "I agree with you, though some white men are no better. Now, you're a smart boy. By this time, you must realize you can't go on living like this. These Kiowas will soon be hunted down and shot by the white soldiers, because they've been raiding and killing and kidnaping through the Panhandle. Your mother needs you, and you should go home to her. That would be a really brave thing to do."

"Blue Flower's very kind to me, and Wolftooth is much better than Froleiks. They won't let me go away, though. I—well, I would if I could."

"Good. Then listen very carefully. There will be a big celebration tonight, it will last till dawn, dancing and feasting. Blue Flower and Wolftooth will take part in it. When you have seen it begin, go quietly back to your lodge. I'll come for you, and I'll have a pony for you to ride. I think we can slip away through the forest. Will you do this?"

"Yes. I'll be ready when you come."

Sundance was relieved. He strolled to Tall Tree's lodge. He made up his roll, and found some dried strips of meat and some pemmican in a deerskin bag. He ate something, and then sat, watching the preparations in the center of the village. Tall Tree was talking with Wolftooth and other warriors; both Blue Flower and Star Eyes were busy with the squaws.

Sundance knew that if he failed and the Kiowas

caught him as he fled with Roland, nothing could save him, not even Tall Tree.

ELEVEN

Such celebrations were an integral part of Indian life. Dances were considered vital; there would often be dances before a band of warriors set off on a raid or intended battle, as good medicine, the shamans praying for success and offering charms to protect a brave from death at enemy hands.

He saw Roland and some other boys near the spits, and they were begging treats from the cooks, who smiled and handed them choice pieces of the meat. That was good; Roland would be fed. Maybe he figured he'd better eat early, if he went with Sundance.

Then Sundance saw something else. A couple of the Kiowas brought out a keg, no doubt stolen at a ranch in a raid on the Panhandle. If it contained strong liquor, the Indians would loose their self-control entirely.

Tall Tree signalled to him, and Sundance joined the group of squatted Kiowas. A tin cup had been filled from the keg, and was being passed around the circle. When it reached Sundance, he took a sip. It was fiery, Texas "redeye," cheap whiskey served to cowboys in the saloons. It burned his throat, and he drank very little; strong drink had the same effect on him as it did on other Indians: it made him crazy.

Once they'd had a few rounds of the redeye, the Kiowas would lose all caution. Even the wily Apaches could not hold the white man's poison brews.

Dark fell over the great forests, and the fires were built higher. The din from the village increased, and the Kiowas began boasting and gesturing, playfully threatening one another. Sundance slowly withdrew from the circle. He went toward Blue Flower's lodge, ducking under the entrance flap. He shoved his roll under the back of the tepee, and crawled under. Watching carefully, he flitted along until he was in the shadows near the creek.

Eagle was nearby. Sundance cinched on his saddle, and fastened his parfleche bags and bedroll to his rig. He led the appaloosa to the far side of the stream, and signalled him to stand. Sundance was an expert horsethief; he'd won a couple of eagle feathers in his warbonnet for this. The herd boys were about a quarter mile up the line from the camp. He crept in without a sound; the boys were looking longingly toward the great fires in the village center. They would be relieved after a time by others.

It was an easy matter for such an expert as Sundance to catch up one of the Indian ponies. The mustang had a rope loop about its neck, and it followed him obediently as he led it back into the woods and across the creek.

To be sure the mustang wouldn't sound off, he tied a bandana around its nose, and took it near to the point where he had left Eagle.

Now he must wait, wait until the Kiowas grew entirely engrossed in dancing and feasting. The redeye whiskey had had its evil effects, and some of the braves were giving war cries and firing guns into the air.

Sundance watched; he could see most of the proceedings. A warrior leaped up and began dancing; he gesticulated; crying out, acting to show his people how he had attacked and slain, then scalped a white man during the raid. Another joined him, and the scalps taken in the Panhandle were waved about on lances for all to see. Squaws applauded; before long, men and women were dancing about, the hide drums banging a rhythmic beat. Rattles were being shaken, and the din began to fill the night air.

Sundance squatted in a black shadow cast by a tall oak. Before long, the party would reach its peak although it would continue most of the night. It was almost time to go for Roland.

Suddenly, Sundance caught a foreign sound. It came from the direction of the pony herd, and he thought it was a choked-off cry. A pistol shot came next, but it was drowned out in the din of the howling Kiowas.

A chill foreboding struck him, and he turned and raced toward Blue Flower's lodge.

Before he reached the tepee, heavy volleys rang out. Glancing over a hunched shoulder, Sundance saw uniformed troopers rushing in from three directions. They were firing indiscriminately, shooting

134

down braves, women, children. Several lithe, half-naked figures ran among the tepees close to the in-trail; they had lighted pitch brands, and were setting fire to the lodges.

At the same time, they poured slugs through the hide. They were Indian scouts, Rees and Snakes employed by the Army.

They were just as expert at tracking as any other Indian tribe, and they would have picked up the trail of the hostiles and followed it like bloodhounds. Sundance recalled that there had been 300 Rees and Shoshones with General Crook, Three Stars, shortly before the Battle of the Little Big Horn, when Crazy Horse had decoyed Crook's advance guard into a trap on the Rosebud River. Crazy Horse had administered a smarting defeat to Three Stars, and Crook had been forced to retreat to Bear Creek and await reinforcements.

The Rees had led the white soldiers to the Kiowa village, hidden deep in the forests of Indian Territory. The noisy, great victory celebration, plus the blazing bonfires, had completed the betrayal of the Kiowas' position, and the hostiles had neglected their usual precautions in guarding the approaches. This all became clear in Sundance's quick, analytical mind.

Now he realized what he'd heard just before the main attack began. The herd boys had been snaffled and the pony herd would have been stampeded to prevent possible escape by Kiowa braves. A few Rees had stolen upon the boys, who would have been looking toward the center of the village, wishing they were there, and seized them; one had been strangled just as he started to call out. Seizing the pony herd was one step in attacking an Indian encampment; the white-eyes had learned that.

The troopers had quietly moved into position, with any sounds they might have made lost in the Kiowas' own whoops.

The soldiers ran in; they were dismounted cavalrymen, afoot so they could operate more effectively here. Led by the Rees and Snakes, they began pouring bullets indiscriminately into the crowd about the fire and through the nearest lodges, killing men, women and children.

He was almost at Blue Flower's lodge when he saw Roland emerge from the entrance flap, stand up and stare toward the awful scene beyond. Sundance drove forward, and knocked the boy flat.

"Keep down," he warned. "The soldiers are here!"

Roland was gasping with horror. "I—I just saw them shoot down Wolftooth—!"

"Quick, crawl under the back of the tepee," ordered Sundance. "They'll kill us and we can do nothing to help now."

Roland took a last peek from the front entry, and he said, "Here comes Blue Flower—she's hurrying to help me—" He broke off with a great sob.

Sundance looked out. Blue Flower was halfway to her lodge, as she tripped and went down to her knees. As she struggled to her feet, more bullets found her, and then she fell, lying quite still, her arms stretched toward the tepee where she had known Roland was sleeping. Her last thought had been to save her new son.

Sundance shoved the boy; he knew they had no moment to waste in mourning. Bullets were already snapping through the dried hides of which the lodge was formed. "Stay very low, Roland," he warned again, pushing the lad out ahead of him. Roland was weeping at the awful sights he'd looked upon.

Behind the tepee they were in dense shadow, away from the dancing ruby glow of the fires. The noise was deafening; some of the warriors had snatched their lances and a handful attempted to counterattack. Keeping Roland ahead of him, to protect him, Sundance glanced back. He saw his friend Tall Tree drive his lance through a Ree scout, but then Tall Tree was riddled with lead and fell back into the blazing bonfire behind him.

At the same moment he saw a naked, Indian torso gleaming with tallow, a feather in his black braids, streaking toward Blue Flower's lodge. It was a Ree scout; he gripped a blazing pitch torch in one hand, and a carbine in the other. He was burning the tepees.

As Sundance, Roland close before him, came from behind the lodge, the Ree sighted them and uttered a warwhoop of triumph. The Ree had the carbine pointed down and it took him a moment to raise the rifle and aim. Sundance dropped to his knees; the ivory-handled Colt flashed out and he pulled trigger, his human target outlined against the red glow from the center of the village.

The Ree's carbine belched flame and metal but the bullet flew high, for the savage had been hit by the heavy .45-caliber slugs. He fell heavily on his face, the torch flying from one hand, the carbine from the other. He twitched but he was dead, for he'd caught one of Sundance's bullets in the heart.

Sundance pouched the revolver and snatched up Roland, running swiftly toward the creek. Whatever sounds the explosions of the carbine and Colt had made were lost in the general hubbub. The troopers and other scouts were still pouring bullets into any living enemy they saw; the hostiles would be wiped out, few if any captives taken. The attack had come so suddenly that Sundance knew the three white women, being held off from the village, would be saved, for the Kiowas wouldn't have had time to kill them.

Roland was slim, and Sundance easily carried him; he could feel the boy was crying, racked by sobs.

Now he had reached the bank of the creek, and went down into the stream, splashing through the shallow water.

He knew he had only minutes to effect escape. If the Rees sighted him, they'd be after him, but they were busy in the village, and many of them were taking Kiowa scalps, whooping it up in triumph. They hated their hereditary enemies; the Cheyenne, the Sioux, the Comanches and Kiowas, and had thrown in their lot with the white invaders, along with the Snakes and the Pawnees.

The big appaloosa was waiting for him, and nosed at him; even Eagle didn't like such fires as were raging now in the Indian camp. As for the Indian pony, the creature was dancing about, almost frantic, trying to break free from the stout rope which Sundance had fastened to a tree limb. He was glad he'd taken special pains to make sure of the tie.

He undid the rope, quieting the mustang, but careful to hold him. "Jump on, Roland," he ordered. "Hold tight to his mane so he doesn't throw you off. The fire has terrified him."

The youth was an accomplished rider. He was astride the pony in a single leap, and grasped the mane, staying low over the withers. Sundance kept hold of the lead-rope, and mounted the tall appaloosa. The Indian pony danced, still worried about the fire, which seemed to be spreading into the nearby woods. The lodges, for the most part, were blazing like torches. The bodies of dead and wounded Kiowas were being thrown onto the bonfire, along with lances, bows and other captured items, though the Indian scouts might keep whatever they fancied. They'd scalped many of the Kiowas . . .

Sundance kept a short rope on the Indian mustang as he started Eagle along the creek, heading roughly southeastward according to its general course. He stayed in the shallows, and had to move slowly. The pony seemed to take comfort in being close to the big stallion. Horses were like that, Sundance knew, and so were most animals, including men, enjoying and finding strength in the company of their fellow beings.

He knew he must put as much distance as he could between the village and himself. The Ree scouts might pick up his trail and try to follow it down the stream. But it would be daylight before they could do this, and Sundance had a few hours in which to escape.

Glancing back, he could still see the red glow from the burning Kiowa encampment. But he could no longer hear the noises, just an occasional dim gunshot.

This, he knew, had been and would continue to be the fate of any redmen who fought to defend their hunting grounds and their tribes against the ruthless whites. He'd seen what had happened to the mightiest of all tribes, the Teton Lakotahs and their blood brothers, his own tribe, the Cheyenne. Even Joseph and his Nez Percés, who had never before fought the invaders, were about to be conquered.

They had to travel very slowly. Sundance was closed in by the black walls of the growth along the stream. When he glanced up, he could see the narrow break in the foliage over the creek and a few stars twinkling faintly high in the clear sky.

The small river was flowing in the general direction he wished to go, and he would keep moving until daylight.

Suddenly, he heard a splash and the Indian pony jerked on the lead. Roland had fallen asleep and slid off his mount's back.

He stopped, picked up the wet boy, who had been awakened by the sudden jolt and the cool water. He decided to carry Roland ahead of him. The appaloosa was extremely strong, and Roland didn't weigh much. At this slow, easy pace, it would prove no strain on Eagle.

Roland leaned back against him and he put an arm around the lad. He had become fond of Simone's son, and thought that if he had a son of his own, he'd want him to be like Roland, brave but not cruel, and clever enough to get along with all sorts of people. He had certainly charmed all the savages he'd met.

Eagle plodded along through the shallows, avoiding branches and large boulders. Sometimes the water reached his belly, usually it was only knee-deep. The Indian mustang had quieted and came along obediently.

Before long, he felt Roland relax, warmed by contact with his tall friend's body. The boy was exhausted, nervously as well as physically. He'd evidently come to love Blue Flower and her husband, who had been so good to him. His Kiowa boy pals, too, had been killed, and it had been a bad shock.

A man of steel, Sundance kept going. But the river began to deepen, and he looked ahead. There was a wide pool, made by an old beaver dam in the creek. Above, he could see more of the night sky, and he found the North Star. There was a chunk of moon low in the heavens.

He stopped, and the horses put down their noses to drink. Sundance lifted Roland off; the boy half awoke, asking sleepily, "Where are we—?"

"We'll rest a while." Sundance got down, knee-deep in the water. He backed into the bushes and broke a way through into a small clearing. Black spruce grew far back, thrusting up, but there were cottonwoods closer to the river.

Roland's scant clothing was almost dry. Sundance put him down and found his bedroll. He spread a blanket, and rolled the boy in it. Then he drank and washed dirt from his hands and face. He found a hardtack and bag of pemmican in a saddlebag; he needed food to keep going.

After this, he told Eagle to stand, and looked for a way around the wide, deep beaver pond. He soon came upon an animal trail which more or less followed the course of the river. This should do for the time being.

Returning, he rested beside Roland, letting him

sleep for a while.

When he wanted to go on, he decided to leave the blanket wrapped around the boy. The air had cooled, and he could carry Roland easily enough before him. He was soon ready to start, and lifted Roland up, mounting Eagle. With the Kiowa mustang in tow, he walked the appaloosa along the narrow track, and soon bypassed the pond. He heard the sound of the waterfall over the low dam.

An owl hooted in the distance, and he heard other familiar noises in the wilderness.

Sundance knew approximately where he was. After another hour's ride, he came out of the woods to a more or less open stretch of country, one of the cattle trails through Indian Territory from Texas to Kansas railheads.

Here he could make better time and increased the pace to a lope, the appaloosa's long, powerful stride bridging the distance.

He was still in the open when he saw the first touch of the new day ahead. He'd seen no lights of habitations, but he'd feel safer when he could get into the forests again. By guess, he believed the Osage village wasn't more than a couple of hours ahead.

If he could find his friend Buffalo Killer, and the other hunters, Loves Many Squaws among them, they'd help him, giving Roland and Sundance food and shelter.

Crimson streamers of the rising sun showed in the sky as he reached the denser woods. Yes, Indian Territory abounded in fine trees, pine, oaks and other hardwoods, invaluable to man. They not only offered comfort and safety to the Indians but they also made a habitat for the deer, antelope and other animals which were the main meat supply for the redmen of the Nations, the buffalo having been wiped out on the Great Plains by the greedy whites.

Finally he reached the temporary camp where he'd first encountered Buffalo Killer and his party who'd been after bison. They had left, of course. But in Indian fashion, they'd left signs pointing to the direction they'd taken. Sundance got down, and now the light was good. Roland was awake, and he stretched himself, saying, "I'm hungry, Sundance." Sundance gave him the bag of pemmican. "It's good," he said, and Roland began stuffing handfuls in his mouth.

Sundance began casting around. Soon he found two small pheasant bones formed in an arrow. This was a pointer; any Indian hunting his friends would know which way they'd taken. By now, any tracks Tall Tree's party might have left would have been obliterated by wind and rain.

When Roland was ready, both mounted, the boy on his pony. Sundance tied the lead-rope to his high horn, leaving some slack so the mustang could follow along. He found a faint trail and rode in the direction the bird bones indicated.

Halfway through the morning, the sunlight patching through breaks in the forest, he reached the Osage village site. But it had moved; he could see the spaces where the tepees had stood, some buffalo bones picked over by scavengers and left by the Osages. There were blackened spots where the cookfires had been, some rusting tins, and white man's supplies which the Osages had bought at the stores.

Again, he searched for pointers. He found a fresh blaze on a large pine tree trunk, and remounting, pushed on with Roland in tow. Around noon, the air warm now, growing hot, he reached the main Osage village.

Dogs barked at the newcomers, and Indian boys threw stones at them, driving them off. The Osages were at peace, and weren't raiding or looking for trouble.

And soon, Buffalo Killer hurried from his lodge to greet him, a broad grin on his face. The chief called to older boys, who took the horses off to care for them, while Sundance and Roland were escorted into the village.

Sundance must sleep, and eat. Then he intended to proceed to Tahlequah, and after that, would head for Fort Smith. By now, a reply to his message should have reached Arkansas from Washington, and Tall Littleman would have it, the answer to the mystery Sundance must solve.

TWELVE

Sundance and Roland remained in the Osage village for two days, resting, feasting. Thanks to Sundance's reputation and Buffalo Killer's friendship, the tall Cheyenne was most welcome. And the Osages knew Roland, who had stayed with them for a time, before he'd run away, since he had refused to go back to Fort Smith.

The Osages had plenty of meat and other foods, and they pressed the best of everything on their guests. The Principal Chief of the Osages welcomed Sundance and smoked a pipe with him. The Chief's name, in English, was Strongbow, and with Buffalo Killer, they listened with deep interest as Sundance recounted his adventures in the Panhandle of Texas when he'd been on Roland's trail.

They exclaimed, shaking their heads sadly, as Sundance told him how the soldiers, led in by Ree scouts, had savagely wiped out the Kiowa village. But that, said Strongbow, was the way of the white-eyes. They killed the Indians as though they were so

145

many vicious beasts. It was an unhappy matter, and the Osages had long ago decided they could do no more fighting because the whites were as numerous as the leaves on the trees and the blades of grass in the springtime. And they had far more powerful weapons and could completely wipe out the Indians when they wished to do so.

Roland had changed, Sundance noted. He was subdued, and seemed to have lost his boyish notions about Western life and the Indians. What he'd seen at the massacre of the Kiowas had shocked him, made a deep impression on his youthful mind. He no longer cared about putting on the performance which had so amused the red men.

Eagle and the Indian pony had rested and grazed. Sundance thanked his hosts, and so did Roland; the two rode off from the Osage village in the morning, and Sundance hit the trail to Tahlequah.

The big man rode ahead. He'd cautioned Roland that at signal, the boy was to draw off the trail and keep silent; he must put a hand over the mustang's nose so the pony wouldn't sound off in case other horses were coming.

They were still a few miles west of Tahlequah when Eagle rippled his sleek hide; and Sundance, too, heard riders coming toward them. He immediately swung around, signalled to Roland, who was a short distance behind. They hid in the woods off the track, and watched as three heavily armed whites rode by; the men were talking but Sundance couldn't hear what they were saying. They weren't deputy marshals from Fort Smith, but they had a hard, tough look to them. Probably they were some of the blood-money hunters still searching through the Nations for the Indian with the flaxen hair . . .

Close to the Cherokee center, Tahlequah, Sundance left Roland in the forest with the horses, warning him again to stay quiet.

The Cherokee settlement seemed to be in a normal state of activity. As he carefully reconnoitered, Sundance saw no sign of white visitors. Boys were playing, old men sat in the shade, smoking and chatting, while the squaws were busy as they always were. Sundance recognized the young girl he'd saved from the rapists; she was helping her mother and seemed to be all right.

He went closer to Our Wise One's lodge. After a time, the Principal Chief came out into the sunshine. Sundance tossed a pebble which rolled in front of the Chief. It was signal enough; the Chief turned and came slowly toward the woods.

Sundance called softly to him, and Our Wise One joined him.

"Did you find the boy?" was the Chief's first question.

"Yes. He's nearby, waiting. Is it safe to come into the village?"

Our Wise One nodded. "Yes. But it's best you hide in my lodge. I'll lift the back flaps and you can bring the white boy in that way. Then we can talk more."

Sundance agreed. The Chief went back into the clearing, and Sundance returned to Roland. Not far off was a small brook and here they unsaddled Eagle, tethered the Indian pony so he could drink and graze. Sundance hung his roll and bags in a nearby tree, and led Roland through the woods.

Our Wise One had raised the rear of the tepee,

and they soon were safely inside. The Chief's wife had already fetched in food and drink, goat's milk for the boy, meat and bread, and some cans of peaches.

Roland was weary, and stretched out on a bear-skin mat to nap. Sundance and Our Wise One smoked and the Chief told the guest that there had been several parties of whites who'd asked about him, as had the two toughs who had nearly raped the Cherokee maiden.

None had been officers from Judge Parker's federal offices in Fort Smith. They had been wolfish, heavily armed fellows, who were plainly blood-money hunters searching for Jim Sundance so they could claim the rewards posted by Franz Berger and Adolf Froleiks.

After Sundance had snatched her from the pair of white rascals, the girl had done as Sundance had directed she do. She had gone straight to Our Wise One and told the Chief all that had happened.

So far, no inquiries had been made about the dead men, whom Sundance had carefully disposed of so as to cause no trouble for the Cherokees. Our Wise One had ordered that all squaws who went into the forest to search for food were to stay well away from the trails and always to be close to one another.

Now, Sundance told the Chief what had happened during his search for Roland. He described how he'd met Buffalo Killer and his party returning from the hunt, and had learned that Roland, the white boy, had stayed with the Osages but when they told him he must go home, he'd run westward again, eluding Buffalo Killer's braves who had taken him close to Fort Sill.

The old Cherokee listened with deep interest as Sundance gave him an account of the terrible siege he'd endured in the dry arroyo of the Texas Panhandle, and how Franz Berger, his enemy, had nearly killed him. Then the Kiowa war party had charged out of the sun and Sundance had gone with them to the hidden village in the Territory, learning that a second band had split off, with the white women captives and the white boy.

"The Kiowas will never stop their raids, now the white-eyes have returned their greatest chief, Satanta, to the prison. Satanta will soon die there, for an Indian cannot stand to be penned up in such fashion, and Satanta must stay there for the rest of his life."

The Chief listened with great interest as Sundance told him how the Ree scouts had ferreted out the Kiowa village hidden in the forests. "I'm sure the second warrior band I traveled with wasn't seen and our trail was well-hidden."

"Then, they must have spied the first contingent, with the white women and the boy, and given warning to the soldiers. After that the Rees must have led the soldiers down on the Kiowa camp during the noisy victory celebration," said the Chief keenly.

Yes, a sad tale for the Kiowas, said Our Wise One. He knew how it was. His own people, the Cherokees, had suffered much at the hands of the whites. But now they were at peace and would never again be driven from Tahlequah and their reservations in the Territory.

Sundance, knowing the white men's greed, had private ideas about this, but he didn't voice them. First, he must make sure, and he would soon find

149

out when he contacted Tall Littleman in Fort Smith and had Barbara Colfax's reply from Washington.

"I would like to leave the white boy with you while I go to Fort Smith," he said.

This was worrisome. The Principal Chief had not only himself but his people to think about. But he said, "We can refuse Sundance nothing. But I'll warn him he must play close to camp and I'll keep guards out to make sure no white men come near; if they do, then we'll hide the boy."

Sundance needed sleep, undisturbed rest. He lay on a buffalo robe at the rear of the Principal Chief's large lodge, and relaxed. And soon he drifted off, hearing the familiar sounds of an Indian village outside.

Roland slept near him on a thick fur bed, covered with a warm blanket.

When they awoke, more food and delicacies were pressed on the guests. Sundance smoked another pipe with Our Wise One.

They would spend the day at Tahlequah. Roland went out to play with his Indian friends, both the Chief and Sundance cautioning him not to stray far from the center.

After an hour or two, Roland came into the lodge and sat down. Our Wise One's squaw petted and washed him, and gave him more to eat and drink. Then Roland sat with Sundance and the Principal Chief.

"I'll be glad to see my mother, though all the Indians have been good to me," said Roland. He spoke English, which Our Wise One understood well.

"Then you don't want to be an Indian or an Indian fighter any more?" smiled Sundance..

"No. I will go back to school and learn all I can. I will never hurt an Indian, and I'll do everything I can to help them, for they're my friends."

This pleased both men. Sundance had long before realized that Simone's son was not only a brave boy but a brilliant one, quick to learn, and to charm people.

"I intend to leave you here, Roland, until I see your mother and arrange to return you to her. There are things I must see about before this is done, however. I want you to obey Our Wise One and wait until I come back for you. Do you promise?"

"I promise. And I will never run away again."

"Good. You can go and play again now until it's time to sleep."

Sundance took it easy in the settlement. The Cherokees were an advanced tribe, and had their schools and a church at Tahlequah.

An hour before sunset, Sundance went back to Eagle. He released the Indian mustang Roland had been riding, and the pony walked off, attracted to a band of the Cherokee horses nearby.

Sundance arranged his packs and cinched on his high-pronged saddle. He led Eagle toward the village.

Then he heard a loud voice, a voice he recognized, and he gave a violent start.

"You vill suffer for this, you Cherokee dogs! You haff hidden this white boy, and haff broken the law! I vill see to it Tahlequah is burned to the ground and your chiefs are sent to prison. The rest of you vill be banished to the Dakota badlands. All you miserable flea-bitten redskins vill go there, understand?"

Sundance touched the appaloosa, ordering Eagle to stand and wait.

Then he slipped to the edge of the woods, looking out on the scene.

Our Wise One stood, proudly, his seamed face grave. Behind their Chief a silent group of Cherokee braves and their women and children waited, as the big white man who looked like a grizzly bear hurled threats and obscenity at them.

Franz Berger's bearded face worked with fury, and his cheekbones showed a deep red, for he was flaming with rage as he railed at the Cherokees. Sundance was aware that he could make a great deal of trouble for his friends; with Berger's charges—he'd no doubt say the Cherokees had kidnaped Roland—and with Adolf Froleiks' power, Tahlequah would be in hot water.

He felt responsible too, for he had brought Roland back to the settlement.

Now he reached a point where he could see more. Behind Franz Berger, who stood with booted feet planted wide, was a big bay stallion, rein dropped. On the bay was a Western saddle with a roll at the cantle. There was a carbine in the boot on the right and a high-powered rifle with a belt of ammunition for it on the other side of the saddle.

The bay was heavily lathered, and there were bleeding spur gouges on his handsome flanks, showing Berger had driven the animal to the limit. The stallion's head was down, and his wet sides were heaving.

Berger had Roland by the scruff of his neck, holding the boy tightly as he cursed the Cherokees.

"It was our intention to take him back to Fort

Smith," said the Principal Chief with dignity.

"You old liar, you're a rascal! Nobody vill take a lousy Injun's vord against a white man's.—Keep still, you dirty little devil!"

Roland had kicked Berger in the shin, and the big man slapped him and shook him violently.

Thoughts raced through Sundance's alert mind. In a matter of seconds, he'd figured how it was that Franz Berger came to be there. A Ree or Shoshone scout, working for the Army, had spied the first contingent of Kiowa raiders as they hurried home to their hidden village. The scout would have seen the three white women captives and Roland with Wolf-tooth, who had caught and claimed the white lad. The scout would have rushed to Fort Sill, where the commander had ordered out a cavalry patrol, guided by Ree and Snake scouts.

And Franz Berger, who'd escaped during the battle in the Panhandle, must have arrived at the fort on his way back to Fort Smith, or had pulled in at Sill before the troopers had left to punish the Kiowas. So Berger would have known at once the white boy was probably Roland. Maybe he'd been with the soldiers who'd struck the Kiowas, but he would have stayed well to the rear, with the main force of troopers, so that Sundance hadn't seen him in the mad battle.

Even as he moved, Sundance could guess how Berger had come through to Tahlequah. Finding Roland missing at the Kiowa village—perhaps some of the advance scouts had spied Sundance and described him, so Berger knew who it was—Berger decided that Sundance had escaped with the boy. So Berger had rushed eastward, and seen Roland playing with the Indian lads . . .

Sundance hurried out to the center.

"Berger!" he shouted.

Berger, still holding Roland, swung and recognized his foe.

Sundance kept walking toward Berger, hands swinging easily at his sides. He knew only one of them would leave this spot alive . . .

THIRTEEN

Sundance wore his Navy Colt with the yellowed ivory handle. He had his sheathed Bowie knife, with its 14-inch blade. Berger had a Frontier Model Colt's .45-caliber revolver in an open, oiled holster in his cartridge belt, and a hunting knife in a case at his hip. The two rifles were in their saddle scabbards several paces behind him, so they were of no immediate use to Berger.

As far as weapons went, they were evenly matched. But Franz Berger had a great advantage. He was holding Roland in front of him and Sundance dared not shoot for fear he might hit the boy.

Berger instantly realized this. He'd hit Roland so hard, the lad was dazed, helpless, and Berger swung him around as he turned to face Sundance.

"You're under arrest for murder and kidnaping," shouted Berger. "You Cherokee scum, seize that man and hold him! The white man's law vants him, and he'll go to the jail in Fort Smith and be held there for trial!"

Not an Indian moved. With stolid faces, they stood silent behind their Principal Chief.

"Do nothing and tell your people to do nothing," called Sundance, in Cherokee. "This is between the ugly white bear and Sundance!"

Our Wise One spoke, nodding, and the Indians waited.

They were all aware that only Sundance stood between them and troubles too great to weigh.

The tall man with the set hatchet face and the Crow arrow scar on his cheek walked slowly but steadily, straight toward Franz Berger.

He drew close enough to see the burning, red-rimmed eyes of his foe. Berger must have been riding hard, hurrying on to overtake Sundance and Roland before they could reach Fort Smith and the boy's return to his mother. The condition of his horse showed that.

Sundance's big hands swung easily at his sides. He wore his loincloth, moccasins, and the rattlesnake band around his flaxen hair.

He kept watching Berger's paws. The man gripped the boy; he'd have to let go, with his right hand, to draw and shoot. Roland seemed to be recovering though a trickle of blood came from one corner of his mouth, for Berger had slapped him very hard, driving his lips into his teeth.

Sundance was within a dozen paces of Berger when suddenly the man who looked like a grizzly bear released Roland's shoulder, and Berger drew his Colt, the hammer spur cocking the weapon as it was pulled from the open holster.

Death stared Sundance in the face as Berger deliberately raised the Colt and took careful aim. The gun was pointed over Roland's right shoulder.

The boy reacted suddenly. Berger was holding him tightly with his strong left hand, but Roland could see Sundance coming and he glimpsed the Colt aimed at his friend. He cried out and jumped from the ground, his shoulder hitting Berger's revolver.

Berger's Colt exploded, but Roland's sudden move had knocked it out of line. The heavy .45-caliber bullet shrieked in the air a yard over Sundance's head and drove on across the clearing into the trees around the clearing.

Sundance crouched, knees bent; he launched himself at his enemy, and swept Roland aside. Berger was forced to let go of the boy, who scrabbled off on his hands and knees. The huge man sought to bring the muzzle to bear again on Sundance, but now the Indian was close enough, and he grasped the thick wrist, twisting Berger's arm back, so his fingers relaxed. The Colt roared again, almost in Sundance's ear; his head rang from the violent sound but the bullet plugged into the earth.

Sundance punched Berger in the mouth so hard that his own knuckles were skinned and Berger's lip was split wide open, spurting red blood. The Colt fell from Berger's hand as Sundance knocked it from the man's fingers.

Berger quickly recovered from Sundance's blow. He jumped back, eluding Sundance's followup to the belly. He went into a bear crouch then, eyes narrowing. Sundance was on the balls of his feet, ready to spring like a cougar on the attack.

He jumped in with blinding speed, striking at Berger's jaw again, but Berger was also an expert

157

rough-and-tumble fighter. He pulled his head aside, and Sundance's driving fist slid over the beefy shoulder.

Franz Berger didn't attempt another punch, for now he saw the chance he had been waiting for. With a bellow of triumph, he wrapped his huge arms around Sundance before he could jerk back out of range.

Berger relentlessly applied pressure, hugging Sundance to him. Sundance could smell the rancid, sweaty odor, and Berger's breath was rotten, too. He tried to get a hand under the bearded jaw, but Berger had pressed his head against Sundance's chest.

The giant Teuton lifted Sundance's feet off the ground and increased the pressure. The wind was forced from Sundance's lungs and he kicked helplessly, like a large insect impaled on a pin.

Sundance turned his head as he fought for air. He couldn't reach his knife and Berger didn't go for his, for now he had his enemy in a death grip, and was sure he had won. No man had ever broken from his bear hug.

Berger squeezed even harder, grunting with the effort. Sundance felt something crack in his right side, and he thought his lungs must collapse.

He had only moments, he realized, before he'd lose all his power to fight, and then Franz Berger could kill him at his leisure.

Fighting for his hold on life, Sundance made one final and violent move. He managed to ram his knee hard into Franz Berger's crotch.

Berger muttered a curse at the sudden stab of pain, and the agony of it made him relax his muscles for a moment.

Sundance was able to suck in life-giving air; he kneed Berger again, and was able to whip around to one side, and duck from the embrace of death.

The Cherokees had watched in horror as they saw Sundance about to be killed. Some of the younger men had started forward, but the Principal Chief waved them back, for he was aware this was a struggle of Titans, and such a duel should not be interfered with.

Our Wise One was waging a difficult war within himself, for if Berger won, it would spell terrible trouble for Tahlequah and the Cherokee Nation. Franz Berger would bring all sorts of charges against the Cherokees, kidnapping Roland, harboring Sundance, a fugitive wanted by the whites for murder in Fort Smith.

Teeth bared like a battling wolverine, Sundance whipped the Bowie knife, with its 14-inch blade, from its sheath, balancing on the balls of his feet as he circled Berger. He held the long knife with his thumb along the blade, for ripping rather than for stabbing.

Franz Berger jumped back and drew out his own long knife.

They revolved slowly, always watching one another; Sundance stepped aside as Berger made a thrust at him; he hoped the giant Teuton would drive forward, off balance, drive himself onto Sundance's point. But Berger was too smart for that; he was only testing his opponent and easily avoided Sundance's slash. For such a heavy fellow, Berger was remarkably quick. He'd cooled off, too, knowing he was facing a master equal to himself.

As Sundance made a sudden twist, Berger just missing his thrust, he felt a sharp pain in his side but he could let nothing interfere with the deadly business. He gritted his teeth, ignoring the pain with Indian stoicism.

The Cherokees watched with silent fascination. They knew that Sundance was fighting not only for his own life, but fighting to save the Cherokees, and all Indians.

Sundance was still breathing hard from his ordeal in Franz Berger's bear hug. And Berger too was puffing now, from the exertion and strain. His red-rimmed eyes were narrowed as he concentrated on this life-or-death struggle.

The sun had enlarged to a huge red ball; a strong shaft of blinding sunlight broke through a clearing onto the field of battle, and Sundance slowly maneuvered toward it. Just as he reached it, he made a swift turn, and Berger, intent on the fight, swung around just as suddenly.

Too late, Berger found he was facing the blinding light, and before his eyes could adjust, Sundance made his desperate lunge, straight at the huge belly of his foe.

Berger's knife scratched his arm but it was superficial, and Sundance drove the keen point of the Bowie, the blade sharp as a razor, into the Teuton's guts, ripping upward, twisting with all the power left in him.

Sundance's ruse had worked. He knew Berger was finished, even as his own momentum kept him hurtling forward. Berger's knife arm had dropped; he staggered and as Sundance collided with him, the huge man collapsed, knocked onto his broad back, with Sundance falling on top of him.

A sudden shout rose in the throats of the Cherokee audience as they saw their champion triumph over fearful odds.

As for Sundance, he couldn't find the strength to get up. He lay on Berger's great body; he could feel the man who looked like a grizzly bear quivering in his death throes under him, and the damp, warm blood oozing from the awful wound in Franz Berger's belly.

Berger shuddered once, flexed, then relaxed; the movement more or less rolled Sundance off and he lay there for moments, on his stomach, head turned aside as he kept sucking in air.

The Cherokees came slowly forward, surrounding him, looking down at the dead Berger, and at the great Sundance who had vanquished him.

Finally Sundance found the strength to push himself up and sit, the bloody knife in his hand, blood covering his torso; some had spattered onto his brown cheeks, and the scratch in his right arm seeped a little, stinging him.

He sat there for a while, head down; then he put his arms around his raised knees.

The Principal Chief and two young braves helped Sundance get up. He was unsteady on his feet and his ears roared as blood pounded in his whirling head.

Sundance had had many hand-to-hand fights, but he thought this one, with Franz Berger, would top them all.

A young squaw, the girl he had saved from the rapists, hurried to him with a large dipper filled with cool water from the nearby stream which provided the main water supply for the settlement.

She knelt by him and held the dipper to his lips, and he drank, gulping down the liquid.

Another squaw came up with a bucket and clean cloths, and they sponged him off.

Now, Sundance was able to stand alone. He still gripped the long, blood-stained Bowie knife in one hand; it hung limp at his side.

Sundance nodded his thanks to the women. He turned to the Principal Chief.

"Have your young men wrap the big *wasichu* in his blanket and make sure it is tightly tied around him. Then, before the body stiffens, have them throw him across his saddle and secure him to it carefully, so he can't fall off. He mustn't be found here, or near here, because it would mean trouble for the Cherokees. Make sure all signs of the fight, all bloodstains, are erased.

"Lead the bay stud into the woods along the creek, where he and his burden can't be seen. He is weary and has been driven too hard. He needs rest and water, and should be sponged down, then fed. Stake him most carefully so he can't break free. As soon as I'm rested, I'll take him and the dead man far off, so blame can't be attached to your people."

The big bay stallion had stood, hardly noticing the nearby struggle, for Berger had spurred and driven him almost to death as he'd sped eastward, hoping to come up with Sundance and Roland.

Well, thought Sundance, Berger had caught up with him.

For the last time. The huge Teuton had not only proved extremely strong physically, but he had had a clever mind, and Sundance was the first to admit that Berger had outguessed him more than once.

Head up, the Bowie still in hand, Sundance walked slowly off into the woods. He was caked with drying dust and blood, though the squaws had managed to wipe off some of it with their damp cloths.

He reached the low bank of the creek. Eagle waited nearby and Sundance washed his knife clean and laid it on the grass to dry. He took off his headband and loin cloth, waded into a pool, and lay in the shallows on his back. The cool water slowly flowed over him and he washed himself thoroughly, then drank more, for he couldn't seem to get enough liquid. The scratch in his right arm wasn't serious, and he made sure it was cleansed.

However, when he twisted in one direction, he felt the sudden sharp stab of pain in his side. He ran his fingers carefully down and located it; he decided that Berger had cracked a couple of his ribs in that grizzly bear hug. But he wasn't spitting blood, and he knew that in time, the cracked ribs would heal.

The long bath brought him back to life. He washed his face and shampooed his flaxen hair, getting the grit out of his scalp.

Finally he left the water, and called the appaloosa. He rummaged in a saddlebag and brought forth a small metal flask of whiskey. He poured a little into the arm scratch, and then took two or three small swallows of the firewater.

He could feel the warmth of it flowing through him; it gave him more strength, but he wouldn't drink enough to lose his senses. He corked the flask and put it away.

In the last of the daylight, with the forest growing deeply shadowed, he took out his white man's clothing, a buckskin shirt, Levi's, and a battered felt hat. He donned these, and slipped into his moccasins, which were damp, as he'd had to clean them.

He heard some of the Cherokee men leading the bay into the woods, nearby. As he'd directed, they sponged down the animal, and let him drink sparingly until he'd cooled off. They had a grain feed for him, and they were expert with horses and knew just how to take care of the weary stud.

Sundance spoke to Eagle, pointing toward the other stallion, warning the appaloosa to stay away, for Eagle had caught the other stud's scent, and two stallions might fight.

He could see they had wrapped Franz Berger carefully and tied the corpse with rope over the bay's saddle. He went back to the village and saw they were industriously wiping out all signs of the terrible duel between their friend and their enemy.

Cookfires had been lighted in Tahlequah, and the squaws were now busy; Sundance went to the Principal Chief's lodge, and saluted Our Wise One's squaw, who was off to one side, fixing the meal.

Sundance ducked in under the open flap. The Chief sat, cross-legged on his buffalo robe. He was smoking his pipe, and pointed to the robe near him. Sundance squatted, and Our Wise One passed him the pipe.

"You must eat," said the Chief gravely, "and then you must sleep and rest."

Sundance shook his head and passed the pipe back to his host.

"No, I must ride, and soon, in an hour at the most. The dead *wasichu* mustn't be found here at Tahlequah. I'll take him far away, and get rid of the

164

body so nobody can ever say the man was killed in the Cherokee settlement. But you must make sure the white boy, Roland, stays out of sight. Better have him play off from the center, and always keep watchers out. Why weren't you warned of the big man's approach?"

"He galloped by at such speed, our scout couldn't reach us in time to give warning. He hooted signals, but they were drowned out, and then the white man saw the boy."

Sundance shrugged. There was nothing to be gained by recriminations, but he warned, "There are probably more *wasichun* following after the man who looked like a grizzly bear. You must be very careful. As soon as I can, I'll come back to Tahlequah and see about the white boy. Meanwhile, remain watchful."

Our Wise One nodded; he would issue immediate orders, and he was a good Chief.

Sundance ate a hearty meal. His side twinged when he moved too suddenly in one direction, but the arm scratch had stopped bleeding. And in time, the ribs would knit.

The stars were in the heavens, and a quarter moon was up when Sundance saddled the appaloosa and secured his parfleche bags and bedroll. He checked his Henry rifle, and left it in the boot. The Navy Colt was loaded and in its holster. The Bowie knife had been cleaned and dried, and was in its sheath.

He found the bay stallion rested enough, watered and fed. Berger's blanketed body lay across the saddle, head down one side, legs hanging down the other. Sundance attached a long lead-rope to his own saddle horn, and tied the other end to the bay's bridle ring.

He led Eagle from the trees, and the bay stud came along.

Sundance took his leave of the Principal Chief.

It would be very slow going to stay in the woods en route to the Arkansas, but he intended to take to the wagon road. There was enough light for riding, not too fast, on the wide track, and a cool wind had come up, blowing in his face. He would hear other horses approaching on the road, before the riders would hear him.

FOURTEEN

Sundance rode on through the night hours. The wagon road from Tahlequah to Fort Smith was easy to follow; it skirted the Cookson Hills and lakes, crossing small rivers at fords; there were a couple of wooden bridges over deeper streams.

He encountered nobody, and the air was cool; he felt better, though the strain of the fight with Franz Berger, coming along behind him, dead body tied over the bay stud, had taken a great deal out of him.

As the pace was slow, neither horse suffered, though the bay, like Sundance, had been driven to the limit.

As the first touch of dawn showed in the sky ahead, he went off the highway, down an easy slope at the side of a bridge across a creek. He let the horses drink, then got down and led Eagle along a deer trail which followed the course of the winding stream.

There was good grazing here, and he let the horses eat. Our Wise One's squaw had packed food for him, and he ate, drinking from the clean creek.

The Cherokees had done an excellent job of tying Berger's remains on the bay stallion. The body was completely wrapped, the head and booted feet covered entirely. They'd fastened the neck with rawhide cords passing under the horse's belly and secured on the other side to Berger's ankles. And they'd thoughtfully stuck a short-handled spade into the gear on the bay stud.

Sundance led the bay well back into the woods. He dug a deep grave with the shovel, and cutting the ties, dumped the heavy body, saddle and all, on the ground. He rolled the whole shebang, saddle and corpse, into the hole and covered this with rocks. He threw in dirt, then more rocks, and layered stones and dirt until the grave was full. Very carefully, he strewed layers of dried spruce needles and leaves over the point.

Expert at concealing signs, he erased all traces as he led the bay well off, tying the lead rope on the bridle ring to a tree limb. Then he went back and wiped out the faint tracks left by the horse's shod hooves.

It would be a difficult task for anyone to locate the remains of Franz Berger now.

The day was growing brighter. He led the bay to the creek, where Eagle waited, and making sure he was unobserved, he put both horses into the shallows. Holding to the long rope, he wiped out what sign the horses had left on the bank, and then waded downstream, leading the animals behind him. This would hide the tracks.

Sundance veered away from the beaten road which led to the Arkansas and Fort Smith. It was too dangerous for a wanted man to travel in daytime. There would be riders and vehicles, and he might easily be spied.

He began to work back southeast along the route he'd taken after his close call with the outlaws, Pop, Cappy and Harry. This meant he must avoid high points and long runs in open country, where he could be easily spotted.

Later in the morning, he went into a hidden camp near a lake shore, watered the stallions, and carefully secured the big bay, who was recovering from the terrible beating and abuse Franz Berger had given him during his run from the Kiowa village.

The bay began to show signs of hostility toward Eagle, and the appaloosa was a fighting stallion, too. Such animals would sometimes fight like hell over a harem of mares. Berger's critter trumpeted challenges at Eagle, rearing up, tossing his handsome head, and twice he grew so noisy that Sundance had to muzzle him, tying a bandana about the bay's nose. For the sounds could attract the attention of men from a long distance.

To be on the safe side, Sundance left the spot and went on for several miles, until he found another good place to throw his bedroll. He dozed for three or four hours; the sun was high and warm, but it was cool enough in the shadowed woods.

He was close to the reed-ridden shore of a lake, and an intermittent breeze gusted and waned. Near dusk, the bay began really kicking up. His hooves, beating into the ground, startled Sundance, who threw off his blanket and stood up. The big bay was dancing around, uttering muted calls, baring his teeth, and jerking so hard on his tether rope that he shook the tree to which he was secured.

Eagle, too, seemed most uneasy. He pawed the ground, and his eyes had a crimson glow in them; he'd make false passes at the bay, and Sundance had a difficult time soothing his trained horse.

Eagle kept raising his head and sniffing the air.

Sundance quickly found the answer to the stallions' excitement. Going to the shore of the lake, he sighted a band of horses, all of them unsaddled, standing kneedeep in the water to drink. They were, he decided, a bunch of stray or wild mustangs. And on the higher bank, where he could watch over his harem, stood a powerful pinto. He was the master of the mares, and he was looking across the lake toward the point where Eagle and the bay stood; both stallions were a natural challenge to the pinto.

Then the pinto spied Sundance on the other shore. He trumpeted to his harem, waded in and began nipping at their rumps, driving them from the water.

It was a familiar sight; Sundance had often seen such bands in the great wilderness which had been his home for so many years.

He hurried back. The bay seemed almost insane, pulling back on his tether, kicking and rearing. Sundance went to the animal, unbuckled the bridle strap and ripped off the muzzle, turning the bay loose.

Eagle started for his rival, but the bay had his mind on the mares; as soon as he found he was free, he shook his long mane, trumpeted again, and picking up speed, went galloping off around the lake.

Sundance held the appaloosa, petted him, soothed him.

It had been his intention to turn the bay stallion free before long, anyhow, and hope the horse wouldn't return to Fort Smith. Certainly, the bay couldn't have had any affection toward Franz Berger, who had treated him so brutally, and as Berger had only come to the settlement in order to assist Adolf Froleiks, no doubt the bay had originally come from some distance away.

This was the best thing that could have happened; the bay would follow the mares, and challenge the pinto for the harem. If he won, he'd never go back to civilization until trapped. If he lost the fierce battle, the bay might be killed or he would hunt for another bunch of mares.

Sundance attached a heavy stone to the bridle and sank it in the shallows among the reeds. He was rid of all signs of Franz Berger and Berger's mount.

He saddled Eagle, soothing his friend, fixed his packs and roll, and hurried on around the south side of the lake, following a faint animal trail. The commotion might have attracted men within hearing, and he wanted to avoid any possible trouble.

He mounted and rode slowly out of the lake valley, over a wooded saddle to the next depression. Night would fall soon, and he could move more openly and not be seen from any distance.

He paused to eat from the supplies given him at Tahlequah, and then went on, heading for the Arkansas and Fort Smith . . .

The following night, Sundance pulled up on the river separating Arkansas Territory from the Nations.

It was about 10 P.M., and he could see the twinkling street lamps, the bright lights of the center where the honkytonks were open, and many of the homes were still alight. Checking carefully, he took off his moccasins, and rolled up his Levi's. Holding the Henry rifle over his head, he pushed Eagle down the sloping bank into the water.

Eagle swam for a short distance before his feet hit bottom on the other shore. Sundance dried his saddle scabbard and slid the Henry back into the boot. He rubbed his legs and feet and let down the legs of his overalls, tying on his moccasins.

He wore no paint on his face now, but had on his beaded buckskin shirt and the battered felt hat. By back ways he headed for the livery stable where his friend, Tall Littleman, served as night wrangler. He got down in the shadows, signalled the appaloosa to wait, and padded to the front office, checking to make sure there were no customers around.

The door into the front office stood ajar, and he glanced in. Tall Littleman was alone; he sat with his chair tilted back against the wall, and he was dozing.

As Sundance entered, the Cherokee jumped awake, the front legs of the chair clacking down on the rough board floor.

Recognizing Sundance, he stood up, holding out his hands in a gesture of welcome.

"Tall Littleman," said Sundance, speaking Cherokee, "I've been in Tahlequah and have stayed with your Principal Chief, Our Wise One. He is a great man, a fine leader."

Tall Littleman stared at him; he could see that Sundance had recently been in a hard fight. The arm scratch had scabbed over; it still hurt Sundance when he turned too suddenly in one direction, but the ribs were healing, too. However, Sundance had a gaunt look from his long, difficult journey and what he'd gone through as he fought Franz Berger and hunted for Roland, Simone's son.

"Have you been to the telegraph office?" asked Sundance.

Tall Littleman nodded. He had a sealed envelope pinned under his shirt, and he brought it out and handed it to Sundance. In a clear, rounded handwriting, the envelope was addressed, "John Olliphant, Fort Smith, Arkansas."

"Keep watch for me, Tall Littleman, while I read this," ordered Sundance.

He moved to the small desk; the lamp was turned low, and he brought up the wick so he could read more easily, as Tall Littleman went over and stood just inside the door, on guard.

The telegraph operator at Fort Smith had written out the message in the same round, easily read script.

It was a long message, and there were two pages. Sundance scanned it, then read it through very carefully.

And as he studied Barbara Colfax's information, wired to him after she and their lobbyist had made their investigation, the big man's black eyes narrowed and seemed to spark, his face darkening with fury, with hate.

Now he knew.

Sundance never looked for unnecessary trouble, and he killed only in self-defense or for some other very potent reason.

But the information in the message told him he must check Adolf Froleiks, no matter what it might cost him. Sundance would go to any lengths, take any steps, to save what little had been left to the American Indian.

He would not be fighting for himself, but for his unfortunate Indian friends.

Franz Berger was dead. That was something, but Berger had been only a field commander, clever and powerful as he might have been.

Adolf Froleiks was a different matter. Even without Berger, Froleiks would do enormous damage.

For years, Sundance had been wiring large amounts of money he'd earned to Barbara, keeping only a small percentage for himself so he could operate efficiently. Sometimes he would take in $10,000, $20,000, and even on occasion had been paid as high as $50,000 for his dangerous, difficult assignments.

With the money sent to her by Sundance, Barbara Colfax had hired a trained lobbyist to fight for the right of the Indians to exist. In the long reply to Sundance's inquiry, she'd said that thanks to his warning, they'd uncovered what Froleiks planned and had started counteractions, publicity, against the lobbyist hired by Froleiks. They'd found a champion in the Senate and in the House.

"Tall Littleman, I want you to hide my parfleche bags, my rifle and roll in your private loft, keep everything secret. If I don't return, they belong to you." He gave Tall Littleman more money, pressed it on the Cherokee wrangler.

Tall Littleman looked puzzled and worried. "I understand. But—what will the Indians do without Sundance?"

The big man shrugged, grim face set, with the hatchet nose and thin lips. He went off, to fetch Eagle, quickly returning.

He kept his Bowie knife and the Navy Colt with the yellowed ivory handle. Tall Littleman climbed to his loft, and Sundance passed him up his parfleche bags and blanket roll, but left the saddle on the appaloosa, and the coiled lariat on its hook.

He rode off, along a back alleyway, toward Froleiks' house. He turned off twice to avoid passersby, who were going home.

He knew the way well, from his previous runs. Within easy walking distance of Froleiks', he left the appaloosa, ordering Eagle to stay. The stallion would be close, when and if Sundance returned. There was a shadowed vacant lot, with bunch grass in it, where the animal could graze and wait for him. Nobody could touch the big horse unless Sundance told Eagle to permit it.

He reached the rear grounds of Froleiks' without incident. The servants' quarters in the rear were dark; they'd finished the day's work and had turned in. Circling the premises, he saw lights in Simone's bedroom and in the front room where Froleiks usually sat.

The clop of hooves, coming in from the street warned him, and he froze in the shadow. Three riders showed against the street lamp. They pulled up at the front veranda. Two got down and he heard their spurs clank as they crossed the porch. The third man waited outside, holding the horses. He rolled a quirly and lit it; Sundance had a flash of the bewhiskered face. Probably one of Berger's gunhands, he decided.

He padded around the back of the house and came up under one of the windows looking into the office.

The two who'd just arrived were in the room; Froleiks had risen, and faced them. One asked, "Has Berger been here?"

Froleiks seemed in an evil temper. "No, I haven't seen him since he left for the Panhandle. Where is he? I need him."

"Well, we can't figger where he's gone to! We were with him and a cavalry patrol, led by Ree and Snake scouts, and they attacked a hostile Kiowa camp in the Nations. Couple of the Rees claim they saw your son, Roland, and they also spotted Sundance. But when the troopers cleaned out the Kiowa village, Sundance and the boy had disappeared. Berger took off on that fast bay stud of his. He ordered us to follow; he wanted to rush back and see you, for he figured Sundance had your son and would fetch him home."

"Berger hasn't showed," growled Froleiks. "Didn't you see any sign of him on your way through?"

"Shucks, no. We rode fast as we could, but we sure couldn't overtake that bay stud, he's lightnin', and Berger never spares the whip and spurs. We stopped at Tahlequah but the Cherokees claim they ain't seen Sundance or the kid."

"Well, get going, round up your hands and tell 'em to sift through town and watch for Sundance. Hustle."

"Soon as we eat and rest some." The gunny sounded sullen. "We ain't been paid for a month, either. I got a dancehall girl I'm takin' care of—"

Froleiks threw some bills at the man. "Get out,"

he shouted, almost shrieking.

The two picked up the money, shrugged, and left. Sundance watched them riding slowly back to the road.

Now Adolf Froleiks poured himself a stiff drink of whiskey and downed it at a gulp. Then he filled his glass again, and went to his chair in front of the fireplace. He picked up what looked like a telegram and read it, then cursed out loud, crinkled it up in his big hand and threw it into the hearth.

He finished his drink; evidently he'd been at it for some time. When he rose, he was unsteady on his feet. He went to the open hall door and bellowed, "Simone! Come down here at once!"

He went back, sat down, poured another drink, and as he faced the window, Sundance could see his face was crimson with rage, and his lips writhed as though he were in a terrible fury.

Soon, Simone appeared in the doorway. "You called me, 'Dolf?"

"I called you," said Froleiks between clenched teeth. "Come over here!"

Slowly, the pretty Frenchwoman approached her husband.

He glared up at her. He began to curse and abuse her.

"You stupid little fool, look what you've done to me! You sent for Sundance, and that's caused me a great deal of trouble. And to cap it, Sundance's agents in Washington have started counter work opposing me. Now I must hurry to Washington and pay out another fortune to try and counteract what Sundance has done! All thanks to you—"

With a shriek, Froleiks jumped up and hurled the

whiskey into Simone's frightened face. She cringed and he slapped her, almost knocking her down, and as he went for her, the panic-stricken woman turned and Froleiks kicked her as hard as he could.

Simone fled from the room, Froleiks shouting more abuse after her.

Sundance, too, was consumed with fury as he saw Froleiks strike and kick his wife. It was too late to stop what Froleiks already had done; Simone had escaped and returned to her room.

But Sundance's big hands worked convulsively; he could almost feel Froleiks' throat in his trip.

FIFTEEN

The way was clear. Sundance went over the side railing of the porch and silently padded to the front door. Upset and with too much liquor befuddling his brain, Froleiks hadn't bothered to follow the gunhands and draw the bolt. Sundance managed to open the door with scarcely a sound.

In a few swift steps he was in the large front room. Adolf Froleiks slouched in his comfortable chair, staring at the cold fireplace. He didn't hear Sundance coming until he was within a couple of jumps, and Sundance said softly,

"Howdy, Herr Capitan Froleiks!"

Froleiks jumped inches off his seat; he half turned, and his eyes riveted to the grim face, with the thin, set lips, the hatchet nose, the Crow arrow scar on one cheek. He took in the hair, the color of new wheat.

He knew who had come for him. "Sundance! How —?"

"Never mind, here I am." Sundance spoke in a

179

cool, controlled voice. "I've finally discovered exactly what you aim to do with Indian Territory."

Froleiks swallowed; the shock seemed to sober him.

"Let's talk this over, Sundance," he said in a reasonable voice. "What do you want, money? I'll make you a millionaire, you can have everything a man ever hoped for. Work for me, work with me."

"You and Franz Berger accused me of murder. There are "Wanted" circulars posted here for me."

"I'll call them in, say it was a mistake. So will Franz. After all, Berger's the only witness, the only real witness, against you, your accuser. I can make him forget it, Sundance. I tell you, I'll pay you as much as you say. I have several thousand dollars right here, in my desk."

Sundance shook his head, and Froleiks hurried on: "Listen to me, I'll make you a partner, equal with Berger and with me."

"No need to think about Berger, Herr Froleiks. I killed him in a knife duel."

Froleiks gulped again, blinking. "So—so much more for the two of us, then. My friend, there are millions, hundreds of millions of dollars in this. I'm an expert lumberman; I've made fortunes elsewhere, but they're picayune compared to the value of the hardwoods and other timber in the Nations."

"And the Indian Nations? They've been given reservations in the Territory."

"They'll be moved, the Army will do it. They can be settled in South Dakota, the Badlands, or somewhere else. Once the forests are cleared off, white settlers will pay more for the land, don't you see? We can't lose."

Sundance listened in amazement. Froleiks was a first-class promoter, and a real spellbinder. Sundance was fascinated as Froleiks babbled on: "Sundance, you can have Berger's place and more, you have great influence with the Indians, you can smooth the way for us. Call off your Washington lobbyists, they've made trouble already for me. I had enough Senators in my pocket to cinch the deal, but because of your people, they're hedging, and it's going to cost a large amount to bring it off. You're a great man, I'd be glad to have you with me."

Froleiks was offering him the moon with a few stars thrown in. He was a big fellow, with a determined manner; his mouth had a cruel twist to it. His bull throat pulsed, for he knew he was talking for his life. His face was crimson; close up, Sundance saw scars, no doubt received in a saber duel at some German university. He'd been a soldier, an officer, and in his evil way, was brilliant, a man with big ideas. He kept his light-brown hair cropped close.

He paused; his breath came fast as he sought to enlist Sundance, for he divined why Sundance had come in the night.

Sundance said flatly, "I work for the good of the Indians, not against them, as you're doing, Froleiks. Nothing, no amount of money can change this."

Froleiks stood up, always keeping his eyes on his foe. He realized he had failed and that Sundance was going to kill him.

There was a small table on the far side of the chair Froleiks had been sitting in. And Sundance hadn't missed the snub-nosed revolver lying on it. Aware that he was doomed, Adolf Froleiks hoped to snatch up his gun. He could kill Sundance with complete immunity.

It was the only possible move Froleiks could make. Sundance was posted for murder, and it would be self-defense against a wanted outlaw.

With a desperate lunge, Froleiks went for the gun and got a hand on it, but Sundance had launched himself; he had been ready to spring. He knocked Froleiks sprawling and the revolver flew from his grip.

Froleiks tried to shout for help, but Sundance had him by the throat, and only muffled noises came forth. Sundance straddled him, and his fingers closed, tighter and tighter. The man tried to fight, to break the death hold. Froleiks had once been a very powerful young fellow, but high living, over-indulgence in liquor, had sapped much of his strength. His eyes bulged out, his tongue protruded, as the steel fingers crushed in the cartilege of the esophagus.

After a while, Froleiks quit struggling; Sundance held on, kept his strangling hands around the throat for moments after Froleiks was dead. He was in a cold fury and he banged the head on the floor, Froleiks' neck limp, yielding to every movement.

Finally Sundance regained his self-control.

He stood up, listening, in case the noises might have been heard in the rear of the large house, but he heard nothing.

Now he began to work, efficiently, quickly. He picked up Froleiks' gun and put it in a desk drawer. As Froleiks had said, he'd kept large sums of money on hand, to pay for services, and Sundance figured the Indians had it coming; it would replace some of the cash Barbara Colfax had had to expend in Washington fighting Froleiks' machinations.

He dug out Froleiks' wallet; it, too, had a goodly sum of money in it, which Sundance added to the collection. There were also interesting documents, lists of Congressional figures with certain amounts of money after each name.

Sundance found a sheet of paper and pen and ink on the desk. He printed a brief message: "Gone to Washington. A.F." He left this under the inkwell. It was unlikely the printing would be checked, and the note should delay inquiries for some time.

He worked as fast as he could, smoothing out all signs of the struggle; there was no blood, for he had simply choked his enemy to death.

He picked up Froleiks' jacket, and took that. Then he lifted the dead man, grunting with the effort, and carried Froleiks to the side window. Opening it, he pushed the body outside, threw the coat after it.

Listening carefully at the hall door, he heard nothing to alarm him. He bolted the front portal, and after a final check of the room, turned down the lamp and blew it out. He went out the window, feet landing on Froleiks' bulk. He closed the window.

Now he shouldered the dead man and moved off through the shadows. Eagle was waiting in the vacant field where he'd left the appaloosa, and Sundance was glad to throw his burden over the horse.

By back ways, he rode to the bank of the Arkansas. He took off his moccasins and rolled up his Levi's; finding a long branch of driftwood, he stripped Froleiks' corpse, and wading into the shallows, threw the body out, then shoved it into the current with the pole. He sank the clothing with heavy rocks, and went back to Eagle, dried his legs, put on his moccasins and Levi's.

Jim Sundance rode back to Froleiks' home, and left the appaloosa in a small shed off to the rear of the main stable. He went to the front window, opened it, climbed in. The house was quiet. He went up the stairs to the second floor and into the side wing where Simone's bedroom was. He could see a thin shaft of light under the door; he tried the latch but the door was locked, and he tapped very lightly. "Simone! It's Jim Sundance." He kept his voice down.

He heard the bolt slide back, and Simone opened the door. She had on a sheer nightgown, and the lamp on her bed table was turned low. But she hadn't been sleeping; he could see she'd been weeping, and there was a fresh bruise on her soft cheek where Froleiks had slapped her.

Sundance closed the door and bolted it. Then he took Simone in his arms.

"I've come for my reward, Simone."

"Oh, Sundance! I was afraid they'd killed you." She began to sob a little, but it was joy. "You've—you've found Roland?"

"Yes. He's safe and well, and he's in the care of Our Wise One, the Principal Chief at Tahlequah. Tomorrow you hire a carriage and driver, ferry the river, and take the road to the Cherokee settlement. You'll find Roland waiting for you; he wants to come home. He loves you very much."

184

He paused, and then he said, "Simone, you needn't worry about Franz Berger any longer. As for Froleiks, he's suddenly taken off for Washington."

She searched his eyes, but then she only nodded, and he began to kiss her, to run his hands up and down her soft body.

The Frenchwoman shuddered, shuddered with delight, and she responded gladly to the man who was so hungry for her.

Sundance kicked off his moccasins and shed his clothes. He helped Simone take off her nightgown, and held her for a time, then laid her on the bed.

She was as passionate as any woman he'd ever known, and starved for masculine attention. Her body was beautiful, too, and Sundance, on one elbow, admired her charms as they indulged in play.

But he needed her; it was a long time since he'd been with a woman. Simone was ready for him, and responded to the powerful man's vigorous attack, squirming under him, climaxing soon, and then again.

When the man had run his first course, they lay for a time, in each other's arms, their bodies warm and close.

Sundance spent three hours with Simone.

The two sat on the side of the rumpled bed. Simone said, "I want to give you the money, too, Sundance."

"No. Your husband's already paid enough, and what you've given me couldn't be bought."

He began to dress, and told her, "I'll watch for you on the road to Tahlequah. Get an early start, and you'll see your son. When you arrive, pay the driver and send the carriage away. The Chief and I

185

will see you and Roland are returned safely home."

She gave him a long, lingering kiss as he made ready to go.

In the late morning, Sundance, on the appaloosa stud, his parfleche bags and gear loaded behind him, picked up the surrey in which Simone was riding. There was a middleaged, steady-looking man at the reins.

He trailed at a distance, always alert; it was possible blood-money hunters, or deputy marshals might be on the road.

After leaving Simone the night before, Sundance had retrieved his belongings at the livery and said goodbye to his friend, Tall Littleman. He'd crossed the river and slept in the forest till dawn, eaten, saddled up and found the trail back northwest.

He'd cut the main road to the Cherokee village, and waited till he saw Simone's surrey pass, then moved on after her. Close to Tahlequah, he'd circled through the woods, left his horse, and watched the happy reunion between Simone and her beloved son.

As he'd advised, she'd paid and dismissed the surrey, and the driver was on his way to Fort Smith.

Sundance left his hiding place and went into the circle where the Principal Chief's lodge stood. Our Wise One had made Simone welcome, and now he greeted Sundance. Roland, seeing his tall friend, ran to Sundance and the man felt the boy's affectionate admiration.

Well, thought Sundance, he'd cleared up Roland's life for him. Froleiks was gone.

Our Wise One offered Simone and Roland a lodge, and she accepted, thanking the Chief. Sundance, Simone and Roland enjoyed the evening meal.

At dark, with a few lights burning in the village, Roland went to bed. Simone joined Sundance, and they walked together.

He led her through a sylvan path to the brook, and they sat by one another. "What will you do now, Simone?" he asked.

"I'd like to return to St. Louis, where I have friends, and Roland can go back to school. I wish you'd come with us, Jim. I'm not sure why, but I don't think I'll ever see 'Dolf again. I found a note, saying he'd gone to Washington, but somehow, I have a feeling he's left me forever. He has many other women."

"You're right when you say you'll never see Adolf Froleiks again, Simone. He had a grand scheme. He meant to bribe enough venal men in Congress to pass a bill giving him timber and land rights to Indian Territory. The Indians were to be banished."

"I'm hardly surprised. 'Dolf had no mercy for anyone."

Maybe Simone guessed that Sundance had disposed of her husband, but if so, she didn't accuse him. However, he wouldn't touch her again if she felt any repugnance toward the man who might have killed her mate.

But Simone put her arms around his neck and kissed him passionately.

Sundance had told Simone he couldn't live in a

city, that he must continue doing all he could for the Indians. And he knew that a cultivated woman such as Simone Froleiks could never adjust to the rough life of the wilderness. Besides, she had her son to take care of, make sure he was educated and kept well.

Sundance had promised to visit her when he came East; they had said farewell, and he'd seen her off with Roland in a carriage furnished by Our Wise One with an escort of Cherokee braves.

Now, Sundance rode westward again. He'd heard the Utes were in trouble, and perhaps he might help the mountain tribes. The Apaches, too, were being hard-pressed.

For he knew that only death could check him as he grimly sought to carry out his great mission.

THE RIDER OF DISTANT TRAILS

ROMER ZANE GREY

The Rider Of Distant Trails marks the return to print of one of Zane Grey's most memorable characters, Buck Duane, first introduced in Grey's novel *Lone Star Ranger*. Forced to turn outlaw as a young man, Buck later teamed up with Captain Jim MacNelly of the Texas Rangers and proved himself to be the Ranger's deadliest gun.

In these stories, Romer Zane Grey, son of the master storyteller, continues Buck's adventures in Texas and as he takes on outlaws who are terrorizing ranches and towns in this tough cattle country!

WESTERN
0-8439-2082-3
$2.75

GUN TROUBLE IN TONTO BASIN

ROMER ZANE GREY

Gun Trouble In Tonto Basin signals the reappearance of Arizona Ames, the title character of one of Zane Grey's most memorable novels. Young Rich Ames came to lead the life of a range drifter after he participated in a gunfight that left two men dead. Ames' skill earned him a reputation as one of the fastest guns in the West.

In these splendid stories, Arizona Ames comes home to find his range and his family haunted by the shadow of a terror they dare not name!

WESTERN
0-8439-2098-X
$2.75

THE OTHER SIDE OF THE CANYON

ROMER ZANE GREY

THE OTHER SIDE OF THE CANYON marks the return to print of one of Zane Grey's strongest characters, Laramie Nelson, first introduced in Grey's novel RAIDERS OF SPANISH PEAKS. Laramie was a seasoned Indian fighter, an incomparable tracker, and one of the deadliest gunhands the West had ever known.

In these stories, Romer Zane Grey, son of the master storyteller, continues Laramie's adventures as he takes on a gang of train robbers, a gold thief, and a sharp-shooting woman wanted for murder!

WESTERN
0-8439
2041-6
$2.75

BORDER RIDERS

ROBERT STEELMAN

Lieutenant David Pine rode into his hometown after six years' absence to find that things had changed. A shadow of fear hung over the town—fear of the ruthless killer, General Pancho Villa.

When Villa's hell-bent gang stormed in, Pine witnessed a slaughter that sent him thundering across the border after the murderers, and into the hands of the desperado Paco Mora. To save his life, David Pine, U.S. Army, was forced to fight side by side with the most vicious outlaws in history!

Before it was over, Pine would be branded a criminal. He'd spill blood on both sides of the border, as he rode a cruel trail that could lead either to freedom—or a noose!

WESTERN

0-8439- 2059-9

$2.25